JN305005

『ラセラス』受容史の研究

泉谷　寛

溪水社

目　次

『ラセラス』受容史の研究（1）
 Ⅰ．はじめに ………………………………………………………………………………… 2
 Ⅱ．1759（宝暦9）年～1784（天明4）年 ………………………………………………… 2
 Ⅲ．1785（天明5）年～1800（寛政12）年 ………………………………………………… 3
 Ⅳ．1801（享和1）年～1850（嘉永3）年 ………………………………………………… 4
 Ⅴ．1851（嘉永4）年～1900（明治33）年 ………………………………………………… 6
 Ⅵ．N.D.版 …………………………………………………………………………………… 7

『ラセラス』受容史の研究（2）
 Ⅰ．はじめに ………………………………………………………………………………… 22
 Ⅱ．明治期『ラセラス』の片影（補遺） ………………………………………………… 22
 Ⅲ．『ラセラス』版（補遺） ………………………………………………………………… 23
 Ⅳ．普及版 …………………………………………………………………………………… 24
 Ⅴ．合本版，訳本版 ………………………………………………………………………… 25
 Ⅵ．著作集・選集 …………………………………………………………………………… 25
 Ⅶ．ＳＪ書誌 ………………………………………………………………………………… 26

『ラセラス』受容史の研究（3）
 Ⅰ．はじめに ………………………………………………………………………………… 44
 Ⅱ．明治期（1868，明元～1911，明44） ………………………………………………… 44
 Ⅲ．大正期（1912，大1～1925，大14） ………………………………………………… 47
 Ⅳ．昭和期（1926，昭1～1988，昭63） ………………………………………………… 48
 Ⅴ．おわりに ………………………………………………………………………………… 49

『ラセラス』受容史の研究（4）
 Ⅰ．Gwin J. Kolb Collection of *Rasselas* ………………………………………………… 74
 Ⅱ．1759（宝暦9）年～1994（平成6）年 ………………………………………………… 74
 Ⅲ．明治期（1868，明元～1911，明44） ………………………………………………… 79

『ラセラス』受容史の研究（5）
 Ⅰ．E.ホジキン作『「ラセラス」の続編』について …………………………………… 96
 Ⅱ．〈幸福の谷〉について ………………………………………………………………… 98
 Ⅲ．『ラセラス』の家 ……………………………………………………………………… 99
 Ⅳ．アジソン編『道徳雑纂集』について ……………………………………………… 99
 Ⅴ．〈選択〉（Choice）について ………………………………………………………… 99
 Ⅵ．『ラセラス』以前以後 ………………………………………………………………… 101
 Ⅶ．ホークスワス作『アルモランとハメト』 ………………………………………… 101
 Ⅷ．釈迦伝と『ラセラス』 ……………………………………………………………… 102

凡　例

1　本編はサミュエル・ジョンソンの東洋物語『アビシニアの王子・ラセラスの物語』(Samuel Johnson, *The History of Rasselas, Prince of Abyssinia*, 1759) について，その版本を中心に受容影響の一端を調査したものである。

1　本編は平成7(1995)年から同11(1999)年にかけて広島国際学院大学『研究報告』に資料として報告させて頂いたものを一巻にまとめたものである。書誌的見地からみても、多分に恣意的であって興味本位の検索領域をでていない恨みがある。足らざる点は今後に期待したい。

1　『ラセラス』に限らず、ジョンソンの人と作品の受容の足跡をたどるには、新たに公刊された次の書誌文献が有益である。これらと照合することによって本編の不足を補足することが可能である。また、インターネット上の検索によって、米英古書市場に現れる版本を入手することも容易である。

藤井　哲編『日本における **Samuel Johnson** 及び **James Boswell** 文献目録』──1871年から1997年までの刊行書──（福岡大学総合研究所報，第208号，1998）

藤井　哲編『日本における **Samuel Johnson** 及び **James Boswell** 文献目録（追加）』──1946年から2000年初頭までの刊行書──（福岡大学総合研究所報，第234号，2000）

Pat Rogers著／永嶋大典監訳『サミュエル・ジョンソン百科事典』（ゆまに書房，1999）

川戸道昭編『十八世紀イギリス文学集』──明治翻訳文学全集、新聞雑誌編13──（大空社，2000）

川戸道昭編『ＣＤ－ＲＯＭ版・国立国会図書館所蔵明治期翻訳文学書全集イギリス文学編』（大空社，2000）

川戸道昭編『マイクロフイルム版西洋文学移入史料集成』（ナタ書房，2000）

J. D. Fleeman, *A Bibliography of The Works of Samuel Johnson* (Oxford, 2000)

『ラセラス』受容史の研究

『ラセラス』受容史の研究(1)

The Reception-History of *Rasselas*; In the Case of the Editions (1)

　　The present paper is intended to explore the various editions of Samuel Johnson's *The History of Rasselas, Prince of Abyssinia*, and next to try to make some comments on the brief reception-history of this oriental story. Since the publication of 'the little book', as the author himself termed it, *Rasselas* has been well received and translated into other languages and finally deserved to claim the classic tale. These extensive diffusion and the increasing scope of popularity of *Rasselas* over the world will give us the interesting and fascinating success story. The scope I extend in this paper is limited up to 1900 through 18-and-19 centuries from the date of the tale's first appearance in 1759. I also turn to the evidence available in the publications of *Rasselas*. In each classification in my listings, the entries of approximately 30 editions which I have traced, though not comprehensive but only selective, are arranged chronologically by the year of inprintings. It seems safe and just to conclude, when we consider both its public appeal and critical reception of today, that Johnson's little book would remain to be the eternal book in the future.

Keywords：Samuel Johnson, *Rasselas*, 18 century, 19 century, editions, reception-history, bibliography.

　本稿はジョンソンの物語『ラセラス』(1759)のその後の出版状況を紹介し、その受容の一端を検討してみようとしたものである。無論、完璧は期しがたいが、期間を18, 19世紀（1759－1900）に限定し、単行本として出版され、

かつ普及したもののみの内より約30版について調査したものである。18世紀中葉に書かれたこのささやかな東洋物語が時代と国境を越えて愛読されてきた軌跡をたどることはわれわれに大いなる興味と驚きをも与えてくれるものである。

I. はじめに

　ジョンソンの『ラセラス』(Samuel Johnson, *The History of Rasselas, Prince of Abyssinia*, 1759, 宝暦9) は今日においても，古典的東洋物語として広く読まれているものである。この倉卒の間に物した小冊子（a little book）が時代と地域を越えて，広く長く愛読され，物語の古典（a classic tale）へと変貌して行く軌跡をたどり，幾多の人心に与えた影響を考慮することは文化史的視点からも尽きせぬ興味と関心を引き起こしてくれるものである。過去二百数十年間に版を重ねて出版された数も，その膨大さゆえににわかには正確さは期しがたい。[1] 本稿では，これまでに筆者が収集し，あるいは閲読の機会を与えられた単行本（editions）のうちから，18, 19世紀に出版された約30冊をご紹介し今後の検討の資としてみたい。勿論，ジョンソンの作品集（the Works）に収録されている『ラセラス』版や翻訳版は原則としてこれを除き，改めて検討することにしたい。冒頭のアルファベット，Aはジョンソンの生存中に出版されたもの，つまり，1759（宝暦9）年～1784（天明4）年，Bは1785（天明5）年～1800（寛政12）年，Cは1801（享和1）年～1850（嘉永3）年，Dは1851（嘉永4）年～1900（明治33）年，Eは目下のところ発行年不明のものを示し，ついでアラビア数字で年代順の整理番号を付し，括弧中に発行年を記しておいた。これはあくまで時代の思潮を無視した便宜的なものであることもお断りしておきたい。

II. 1759（宝暦9）年～1784（天明4）年

　『ラセラス』初版（A－1）の発行は，1759年4月20日と推定される。[2] 同年6月までには初版1,500部が売り尽くされ，第2版1,000部が出されている。翌年4月には第3版（A－4）1,000部が発行されているから，当初1年間で3,500部が世上に出たことになる。当時としては好調な売れ行きであった。第4版（A－5）は1766年（1,000部），第5版は1775年（1,000部），第6版（1,000部）は死去の前年1783年に出ているから，合計6版，6,500部がジョンソンの生前に版権所有者によって出版されたことになる。この外にも作品集に入れられたものを除いても約40の単行本，翻訳本が出版されている。ロンドンの出版物は即座に踏襲されるのが慣例ともなっていたアイルランドでは，ダブリン版（A－2）は同年に出されているし，さらに1777年，1783年にも版を重ねている。翌年には早くもフランス語版（A－3）がアムステルダムで出版されている。ジョンソンの生存中にはイタリア語，フランス語，ドイツ語，オランダ語訳の『ラセラス』本が出たのであるから，『ラセラス』がヨーロッパを征服した，というボズウェルの言葉も正当と言えよう。さらに，1768年には，植民地大陸アメリカにおいて，最初のアメリカ版『ラセラス』がベル（Robert Bell）の手によってフィラデルフィアで発行され，これがその後のアメリカ版（American editions）の魁となる。

1. A－1（1759）初版
　　THE PRINCE OF ABISSINIA.　A TALE.　IN TWO VOLUMES.　VOL.I./ LONDON: Printed for R.and W.Johnson, in Ludgate-Street.　M DCC LIX.

2．A－2 (1759) ダブリン版

THE PRINCE OF ABISSINIA. A TALE. IN TWO VOLUMES. VOL.II./ DUBLIN: Printed for G.and A.Ewing, and H.Bradley, Booksellers in Dame-street, M DCCLIX. (xii＋262pp. 17cm)

3．A－3 (1760) アムステルダム版

HISTOIRE *DE RASSELAS*, PRINCE D'ABISSINIE. *Par M.Johnson[sic], Auteur du Rambler, & traduite de l'Anglois par Madame B*****. / *PREMIERE PARTIE*. / A AMSTERDAM, Et se trouve a Paris, Chez PRAULT Fils, Quai des Augustins, au coin de la rue Git-ie-Caeur. / M. DCC. LX. (1768, 1787, 1788 edns. Mme Octavie Belot)

4．A－4 (1760) 3版

THE PRINCE OF ABISSINIA. A TALE. IN TWO VOLUMES. VOL.I. THE THIRD EDITION. / LONDON: Printed for R.and J.Dodsley, in Pall-Mall; and W.JOHNSTON, in Ludgate-Street. / M DCC LX. (2 vols. 16cm. vol.1, vii＋159pp.; vol.2, viii＋165pp.)

5．A－5 (1766) 4版

THE PRINCE OF ABISSINIA. A TALE. IN TWO VOLUMES. VOL.I. THE FOURTH EDITION. / LONDON: Printed for W.STRAHAN, W.JOHNSTON, and J.DODSLEY. / MDCCLXVI.

6．A－6 (1783) 6版

THE PRINCE OF ABISSINIA. A TALE. THE SIXTH EDITION. / LONDON: PRINTED FOR W.STRAHAM, J.DODSLEY AND T.LONGHAN. / MDCCLXXXIII. (viii＋304pp. 18cm.)

Ⅲ．1785（天明5）年～1800（寛政12）年

　ジョンソンの死後，1786年には第7版（1,000部），1790年には，第8版（1,500部），1793年には，第9版（B－8，1,500部），1798年には発行部数は不明であるが第10版が出ている。ジョンソン自身から『ラセラス』の第6版を贈られたナイト（Ellis Cornelia Knight）は，この物語の続編として，『ディナバス』（B－7）を書いている。以後，両書は合本で出されることになる。この時期から挿絵が挿入されるようになり，若い読者たちの東洋への思いを駆り立てることになる。外にも次のような版が記録されている。

　　　[Parallel English & German], Metz and Frankfurt 1785, London 1786; Harrison's Novelist's Mag 23 1787; Wenman's edn, 1787, Dublin 1787, Edinburgh 1789, London 1790, 1790; Philadelphia 1791, London 1792, 1793, Wenman's edn, 1794; Literary Assoc, 1795, 1796; Dublin [1795]; New York 1795 (with Dinarbas), Harding's edn, 1796; Cooke's edn, [1797]; 1798, 1799; Cook's edn[1799] etc.[3]

これを見ると『ラセラス』は出版以来，18世紀後半を通して英米いずれかの版が出ていたことになる。これが19世紀前半の大流行へと接続して行くのである。

7．B－7 (1790) ナイト作

DINARBAS; A TALE: BEING A CONTINUATION OF *RASSELAS, PRINCE OF ABISSINIA*. / ——Re*E*tius occupat / Nomen beati, qui Deorum / Muneriobus sapienter uti, / Duramque callet pauperiem pati, / Pejus letho slagitium timet: / Non ille pro caris amicis, / Aut patria timidus perire. *Hor. Lib*. iv. *Od*.9. / LONDON: PRINTED FOR C.DILLY, IN THE POULTRY. /

M.DCC.XC. (xii+336pp. 17cm. 1792, 2nd edn. xii+336pp. 19cm.)

8．B－8（1793）9版

THE PRINCE OF ABISSINIA. A TALE. THE NINTH EDITION. / LONDON: PRINTED FOR J.F. AND C.RIVINGTON, J.DODSLEY, T.LONGMAN, AND G.AND T.WILKIE. / M DCC XCIII. (viii+304pp. 18cm. 10th edn. 1798. viii+304pp. 18cm.)

9．B－9（1794）

RASSELAS, PRINCE OF ABISSINIA: *A TALE*. / By S.JOHNSON, L.L.D. / LONDON: PRINTED FOR WENMAN AND HODGSON, NO.144, FLEET-STREET. / M,DCC,XCIV. (vi+ +155pp. illus. 13cm.)

10．B－10（1796）

RASSELAS, PRINCE OF ABISSINIA. / *A TALE*. / BY S.JOHNSON, L.L.D. / A NEW EDITION, *With ENGRAVINGS*. / LONDON: PRINTED FOR E.AND S.HARDING, PALL MALL, BY M.RITCHIE. / 1796. (236cm. 19cm.)

11．B－11（1799）

THE HISTORY OF RASSELAS, PRINCE OF ABISSINIA. *A. TALE*. / BY DR.JOHNSON. / TWO VOLUMES IN ONE. / "He who reads these chapters, will find that it is not merely a course of adventures that invite him forwards, but a discussion of entertaining questions, reflections on human life, the history of Imlac, the man of learning, a dissertation on poetry, the character of a wife and happy man, &c. It is by pictures of life, and profound moral reflection, that expectation is engaged, and gratifies, throughout this work." MURPHY / LONDON: Printed for the Booksellers. / 1799. (142pp. illus. 15cm.)

Ⅳ．1801（享和1）年～1850（嘉永3）年

　この期間に出版された本には精密な銅版画や挿絵を入れた豪華本もある（C－13）。また長文の序文を付して著者ジョンソンの生涯をも紹介している（C－15, C－16, C－17, C－18）。これは主としてボズウェルの伝記からの抜粋であって，『ジョンソン伝』(1791) の成功とも相乗効果を狙ったものと思われる。また作品に対する批評やコメントをした序文もある。このような版が11版各地で出されている。(Dublin, 1803; London, 1809; Edinburgh, 1812; London, 1815; Ed.Sir Walter Scott. London, 1823; London, 1823; Edinburgh, 1824; London,: Charles Till, 1838; London, 1843; Philadelphia: Hogan and Thompson, 1850.[4] 外にも，Bristol(1802), Cork(1803), Banbury(1804), Liverpool(1813), Leeds(1814), York(1815), Oxford(1816), Lanark(1810), Belfast(1821), Derby(c.1830), Manchester(1845), 'Lundum', Pitman's phonetic edn(1849) の『ラセラス』本が上梓されている。[5] 注目すべきことは，この東洋物語が感性豊かな，そして多分に聡明な少年少女たちの好読物として推奨され，かつ愛読された点である。[6] この書物が後々まで彼等の胸中に追憶の書として影響を及ぼしたのである。ウエイトリィの作品（C－25）はこのような感慨から生まれた産物と考えられる。[7]

12．C－12（1801）

THE HISTORY OF RASSELAS, PRINCE OF ABYSSINIA. *A TALE*. / BY SAMUEL JOHNSON, LL.D. / *LONDON*: PRINTED BY C.WHITTINGHAM, *Dean Street, Fetter Lane*, / FOR F. AND C.RIVINGTON, T.N. LONGMAN AND O.REES, G.WILKIE, J.WALKER, J.SCATCHERS,

AND J.MAWMAN. / 1801. (viii+192pp. illus. 17cm.)

13.　C-13 (1805)

RASSELAS, BY SAMUEL JOHNSON, LL.D. / WITH ENGRAVINGS, BY A.RAIMBACH, FROM PICTURES BY R.SMIRKE, R.A. / LONDON: PUBLISHED BY WILLIAM MILLER, ALBEMARLE-STREET; AND SOLD BY MANNERS AND MILLER, AND ARCHIBALD CONSTABLE AND CO.EDINBURGH.　THE LETTER DRESS BY JAMES BABALLANTYNE, EDINBUURGH. / 1805. (iii+197pp. illus. 27cm.)

14.　C-14 (1807)

RASSELAS: *A TALE.*　BY DR.JOHNSON. / LONDON: / Printed by W.Wilson, St.John's Square, FOR J.WALKER; / J.Johnson, W.J. & J.Richardson; R.Faulder & Son; F.C. & J.Livington; Vernor, Hood, & Sharpe: R.Lea; J.Nunn; Cuthell & Martin; Lackihgton, Allen, 6 Co,; Longman, Hurst, Rees, & Orme; Cadell & Davies; Wilkie & Robinson; J.Booker; E.Jeffery; Black, Parry, & kingsbury; H.D.Symonds; J.Asperne; and J.Harris. / 1807. (127pp. illus. 15cm.)

15.　C-15 (1809)

RASSELAS, A TALE BY DR.JOHNSON, / *LONDON.　Published by Suttaby, B.Crosby & C.Scatcherd & Letterman Stationers Court, and C.Lorrall, Charing Cross,* / 1809. (xxiv+120pp. illus. 14cm.)

16.　C-16 (1812)

RASSELAS, *A TALE.* / BY SAMUEL JOHNSON, L.L.D. / EDINBURGH: PRINTED BY WALKER AND GREIG, FOR JOHN GREIG, 261.　HIGH STREET, EDINBURGH. / 1812. (xii+187pp. 18cm.)

17.　C-17 (1816)　ロンドン版

RASSELAS, *PRINCE OF ABYSSINIA.* / A TALE. / BY SAMUEL JOHNSON, LL.D. / LONDON: PRINTED FOR FC. AND J.RIVINGRON; G.WILKIE; SCATCHERD AND LETTERMAN; LONGMAN; HURST, REES, ORME, AND BROWN; J.MAWMAN; WALKER AND EDWARDS; AND B.REYNOLDS. / 1816. (xiv+205pp. illus. 17cm.)

18.　C-18 (1816)　オックスフォード版

RASSELAS, *A TALE.* / BY SAMUEL JOHNSON, LL.D. / OXFORD, PRINTED BY W.BAXTER, FOR LAW AND WHITTAKER, LONDON. 1816. (xiv+205pp. illus. 17cm.)

19.　C-19 (1817)

THE HISTORY OF RASSELAS, PRINCE OF ABYSSINIA.　*a Tale.* / BY SAMUEL JOHNSON, LL.D. / LONDON: PRINTED FOR JOHN SHARPE, PICCADILLY; BY C.WHITTINGHAM, CHISWICK. / M DCCC XVII. (embellished with engravings, from the designs of Richard Westall. viii+184pp. illus. 17cm.)

20.　C-20 (1819)

RASSELAS, BY SAMUEL JOHNSON, LL.D. / WITH ENGRAVINGS, BY RAIMBACH, FROM PICTURES BY R.SMIRKE, R.A. / LONDON: PUBLISHED BY HECTOR M'LEAN, NO.8, SOHO SQUARE; AND SOLD BY MANNERS AND MILLER, AND ARCHIBALD CONSTABLE AND CO.EDINBURGH. / 1819. (iii+197pp. illus. 28cm.)

21. C－21 (1820)

THE HISTORY OF RASSELAS, PRINCE OF ABYSSINIA. / BY SAMUEL JOHNSON, LL.D. / LONDON: PRINTED FOR J.BUMPUS, 6, HOLBORN BARS; SHARPE, KING-STREET, COVENT-GARDEN; SAMMS; PALL MALL; WARREN, NEW BOND-STREET; AND REILLY, LORD-STREET, LIVERPOOL. / 1820. (iv+140pp. illus. 17cm.)

22. C－22 (1821)

THE HISTORY OF RASSELAS, *PRINCE OF ABYSSINIA*. A TALE. / BY SAMUEL JOHNSON, LL.D. / PARIS, THEOPHILUS BARROIS, JUN.QUAI VOLTAIRE, No.11. / 1821. (vi+215pp. 15cm.)

23. C－23 (1823)

RASSELAS; A TALE. BY DR.JOHNSON. / DINARBAS; A TALE: BEIBG A CONTINUATION OF RASSELAS. / *LONDON*: Printed for C.Rivington; J.Nunn; T.Cadell; Longman, Hurst, Rees, Orme, Brown, and Green; G. and W.B.Whittaker; J.Richardson; J.Walker; Newman and Co.; Harding, Mavor, and Lepard; Kingsbury, Parbury, and Allen; Black, Young, and Young; Sherwood, Jones, and Co.; Baldwin, Cradock, and Joy; E.Edwards; Simpkin and Marshall; R.Scholey; and G.Cowie / By T.Davison, Whitefriars. / 1823. (266pp. 14cm.)

24. C－24 (1823)

RASSELA, PRINCIPE D'ABISSINIA: / TRADOTTO DALL' INGGLESE DEL SIGNOR DOTTOR JOHNSON. / LONDRA: PRESSO G.e W.B.WHITTAKER, / 1823.

25. C－25 (1828)

RASSELAS. BY SAMUEL JOHNSON, L.L.D. / LONDON: PUBLISHED BY JOHN SHAPPE. 1826. (1822, 1828 edns.)

26. C－26 (1835) ウエイトリィ作

THE SECOND PART OF THE HISTORY OF RASSELAS, PRINCE OF ABYSSINIA. / BY THE AUTHOR OF "CONVERSATIONS OF THE LIFE OF CHRIST," "FIRST PREACHING OF THE GOSPEL," &C. / LONDON: B.FELLOWES, LUDGATE STREET. / 1835. (v + 58pp. 14.5cm.)

V. 1851（嘉永4）年〜1900（明治33）年

19世紀後半期の出版本として，ここでは3冊のみしか図示しなかったが，『ラセラス』の人気はこの時代も出版点数から見ると少しも衰えていないことが分かる。とりわけ，英米においては優秀な編者によって注釈が施され，かつ学問批評の対象となってきたことである。計12冊の『ラセラス』が発行されている。(Longmans, London, 1860); Ed.Rev.William West, London, 1869; Yale University, Philadelphia, 1873; Ed.Alfred Milnes, Oxfrod, 1878; Whittaker & Co., London, 1879; Ed.Henry Morley, London: George Routledge & Son, 1884; Ed.Dr.James Macaulay, London, Elliot Stock, 1884; Ed.George Hill, London: Oxford UP, 1887; Ed.Henry Morley, London: Cassell & Co., 1888; Ed.Fred N.Scott, Boston and New York: Leach, Shewell and Sanborn, 1891; Ed.Oliver F.Emerson, New York: Henry Holt, 1895; Ed.Justin Hannaford, London, 1900.[8]）さらに，*Vathek* との合本版（1883），Birmingham版（1898）も追記しておこう。また，注目すべきことは開国後の日本のような遠国において，『ラセラス』大流行が起こったことである。[9]

27. D−27 (1869)

RASSELAS, PRINCE OF ABYSSINIA. BY SAMUEL JOHNSON, L.L.D. WITH AN INTRODUCTION BY THE REV. WILLIAM WEST, B.A., INCUMBENT OF S.COLUMBA'S, NAIRN. / LONDON: SAMPSON LOW, SON. AND MARSTON, CROWN BUILDINGS, 188, FLEET STREET. / 1869. (xlviii+162pp. 15cm.)

28. D−28 (1884)

RASSELAS BY DR.SAMUEL JOHNSON / LONDON GEORGE ROUTLEDGE & SONS, LIMITED NEW YORK: E.P.DUTTON AND CO.

29. D−29 (1896) シカゴ版

RASSELAS PRINCE OF ABYSSINIA BY SAMUEL JOHNSON, LL.D. NEW AMERICAN EDITION / CHICAGO A.C. McCLURG AND COMPANY / 1896. (201pp. 19cm.)

VI. N.D.版

正確な出版年を特定できなかった2書についてはほぼ，次のように推定することが可能である。ナイトの『ディナバス』(1790)は1800年までには4版(1790, 1792, 1793, 1800)を重ね，1820年までには最低6版出ているが，単独で出版されるよりも『ラセラス』との合本で出版されるのが普通であった。これにボズウェルの『SJ伝』に倣った序文を付すのが慣例であった。ナイトのみでは人気不足であるから，ジョンソン，ボズウェルを合わせて読者層の購買欲を刺激しようとする版元の意図が窺われる。アメリカにおいても，すでに1792年に最初の『ディナバス』本が出ているし，1795年には第2版が『ラセラス』との合本で出版されている点から見て，ロンドンで発行されたE−30の本は世紀の転換期前後から1820年までのものと思われる。ボズウェルの序文（実質は5頁）を付したE−31本も19世紀初頭のものと考えられる。

30. E−30 (n.d.)

RASSELAS; A Tale, BY DR.JOHNSON: AND DINARBAS; A Tale: BEING A CONTIUATION OF RASSELAS. / WITH A BIOGRAPHICAL PREFACE. / LONDON: T.ALLMAN AND SON, 42, HOLBORN HILL. (vii+240pp. illus. 14cm.)

31. E−31 (n.d.)

RASSELAS, PRINCE OF ABYSSINIA. BY SAMUEL JOHNSON, LL.D. *WITH AN INTRODUCTION* BY JAMES BOSWELL. / LONDON: WILLIAM TEGG. (xii + 179pp. illus. 18cm.)

NOTES

1) ジョンソン書誌には，William P.Courtney and David Nichol Smith, *A Bibliography of Samuel Johnson*(1925); James L.Clifford and Donald Greene, *Samuel Johnson: A Survey and Bibliography of Critical Studies*(1970) 等があるが，故人となられたDr.J.D.Fleemanの著書，*Johnson Bibliography*の出版が待たれる。わが国においては，京都外国語大学付属図書館，関西大学図書館にジョンソン・コレクションがある。京都外国語大学付属図書館編『京都外国語大学蔵書目録』，巻一　英米書之部−総記・語学・文学−（昭和51年），関西大学図書館編『第17回展示　サミュエル・ジョンソン　展観目録』（平成元年5月）参照。

2) *Rasselas and Other Tales*, ed.Gwin J.Kolb, vol.XVI of the Yale Edition of the Works of Samuel Johnson (New Haven and London: Yale Univ. Press, 1990), pp.xliv-1, 253-58.
3) George Watson, ed., *The New Cambridge Bibliography of English Literature* (Cambridge Univ. Press, 1971), vol.2, p.1130.
4) Edward Tomarken, "A Chronological Checklist of *Rasselas* Criticism 1759-1986," in *Johnson, Rasselas, and the Choice of Criticism* (Univ. Press of Kentucky, 1989), pp.194-5.
5) Watson, p.1130.
6) 例えば，ジョージ・エリオットの『牧師館物語』(1858) に登場するリネット嬢の書棚を飾る装丁本の一冊は『ラセラス』であり，彼女が十代の頃に小遣銭で買ったものである（第三章）。また，『フロス河の水車場』(1860) の主人公マギーも難解な人生書とともに『ラセラス』を読んでいた（第三章）。See James G.Basker. "Samuel Johnson and the American Common Reader," in *The Age of Johnson; A Scholarly Annual* 6, ed. Paul J.Korshin (New York: AMS Press, 1994), p.19: " One finds twelve-and fourteen-year-old children reading their copies of *Rasselas* in early nineteenth-century New England; or a nineteen-year-old plantation belle in Virginia reading Johnson's *Rambler* essays in 1863 to distract herself from the Civil War."
7) See Robert F.Metzorf, "The Second Sequel to *Rasselas*," in *The New Rambler* (January 1950), pp.5-7: "The only copy traced so far is in the Charles Sumner Collection, the Houghton Library of Harvard University." (p.6)　この書については，拙稿「ウエイトリィ作『ラセラス』第二部について」（日本ジョンソン協会『記念論文集』（雄松堂, 1996) で一考してみた。
8) Tomarken, p.195.
9) 拙著『健闘の文豪ジョンソン―明治期「ラセラス」の片影』（渓水社, 平成4年）を見られたい。

A-1(1759) 初版

A-2(1759) ダブリン版

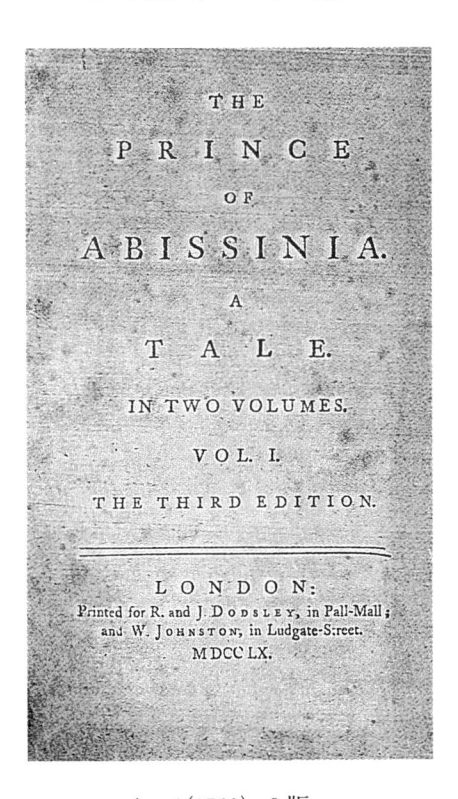

A-3(1760) アムステルダム版

A-4(1760) 3版

THE PRINCE OF ABISSINIA. A TALE. IN TWO VOLUMES. VOL. I. THE FOURTH EDITION. LONDON: Printed for W. STRAHAN, W. JOHNSTON, and J. DODSLEY.　MDCCLXVI.	THE PRINCE OF ABISSINIA. A TALE. THE SIXTH EDITION. LONDON: PRINTED FOR W. STRAHAN, J. DODSLEY, AND T. LONGMAN. MDCCLXXXIII.
A−5(1766) 4版	A−6(1783) 6版
DINARBAS; A TALE: BEING A CONTINUATION OF RASSELAS, PRINCE OF ABISSINIA. —— Rectius occupat Nomen beati, qui Deorum Muneribus sapienter uti, Duramque callet pauperiem pati, Pejus letho flagitium timet: Non ille pro caris amicis, Aut patria timidus perire. Hor. Lib. iv. Od. 9. LONDON: PRINTED FOR C. DILLY, IN THE POULTRY. M.DCC.XC.	THE PRINCE OF ABISSINIA. A TALE. THE NINTH EDITION. LONDON: PRINTED FOR J. F. AND C. RIVINGTON, J. DODSLEY, T. LONGMAN, AND G. AND T. WILKIE. MDCCXCIII.
B−7(1790) ナイト作	B−8(1793) 9版

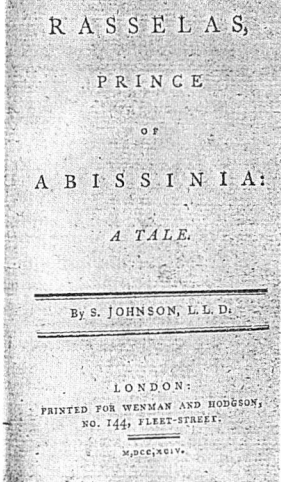

B−9(1794)

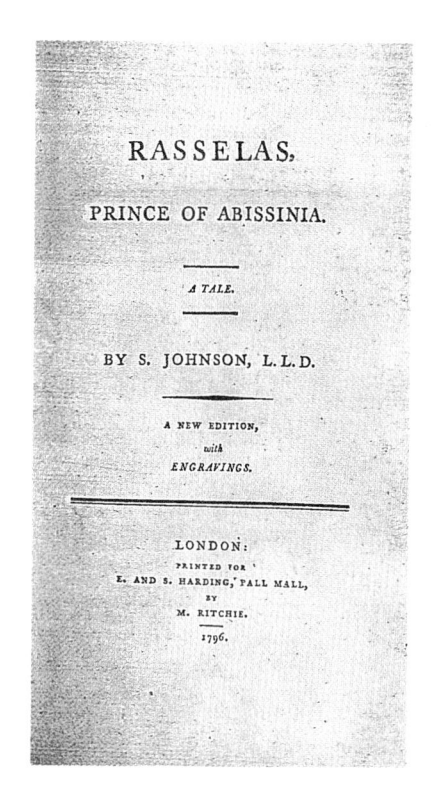

B−10(1796)

B−10(p.11)   B−10(p.70)   B−10(p.98)

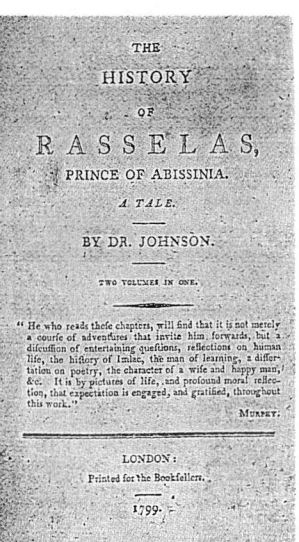

B−10(p.169) B−11(1799)

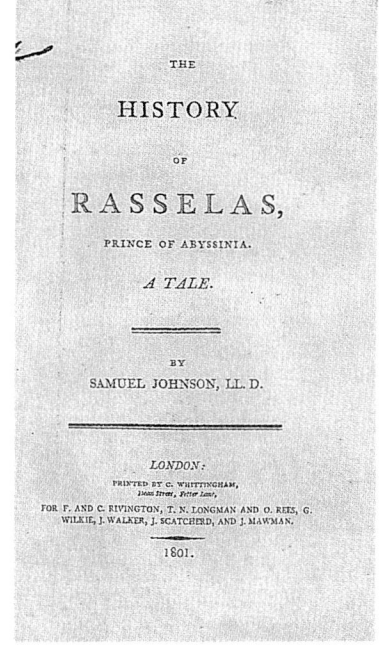

C−12(1801)

C−12(p.17)

『ラセラス』受容史の研究(1)

C−12(p.27) 　　　　　　C−12(p.79) 　　　　　　C−12(p.123)

C−12(p.166)

RASSELAS,

BY

SAMUEL JOHNSON, LL.D.

WITH

ENGRAVINGS, BY A. RAIMBACH,

FROM

PICTURES BY R. SMIRKE, R.A.

LONDON:
PUBLISHED BY WILLIAM MILLER, ALBEMARLE-STREET;
AND SOLD BY MANNERS AND MILLER, AND ARCHIBALD CONSTABLE AND CO.
EDINBURGH.
The Letter Press by James Ballantyne, Edinburgh.

1805.

C−13(1805)

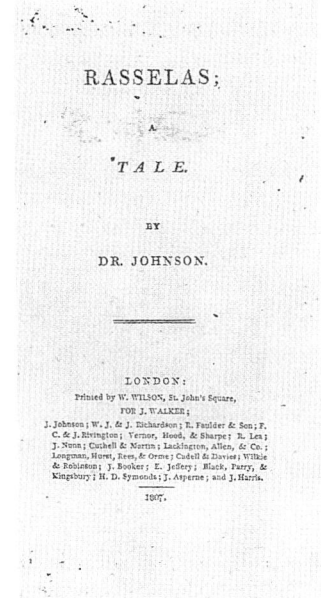

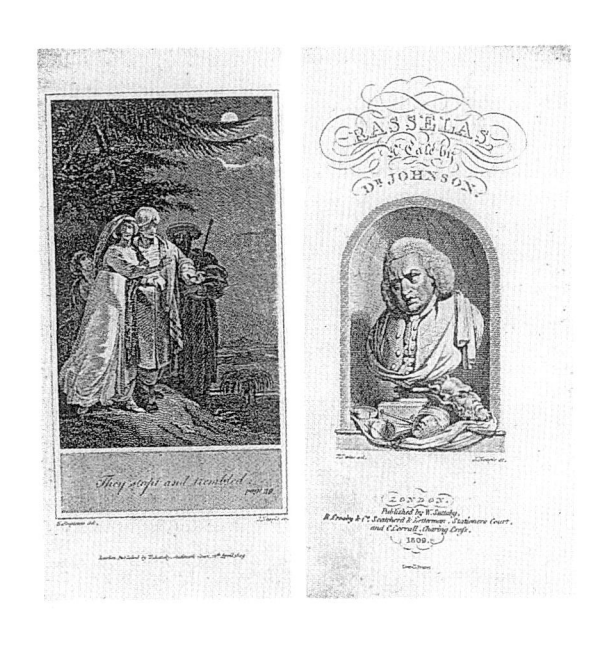

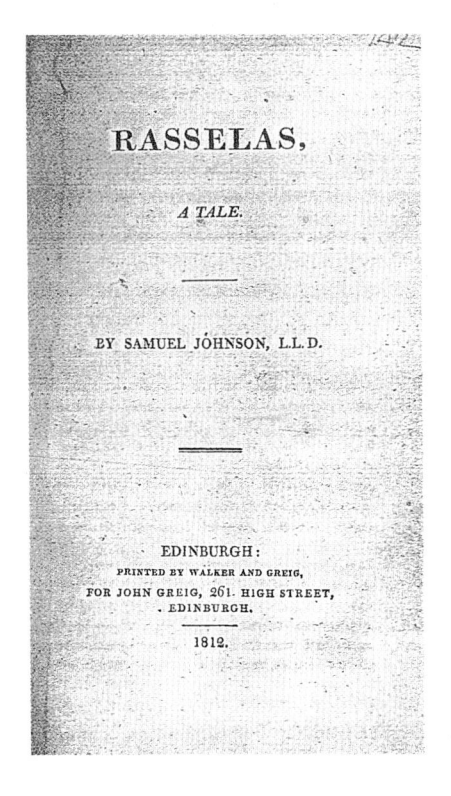

C－14 (1807)　　　　　　　　　C－14 (1807)

C－15 (1809)　　　　　　　　　C－16 (1812)

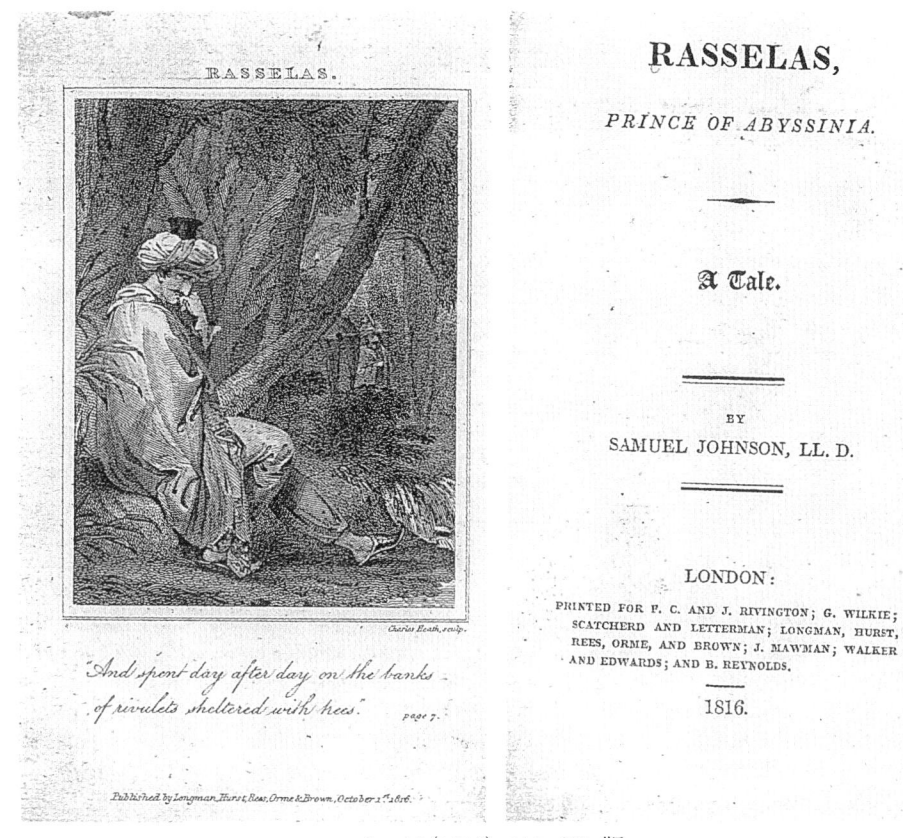

C−17 (1816) ロンドン版

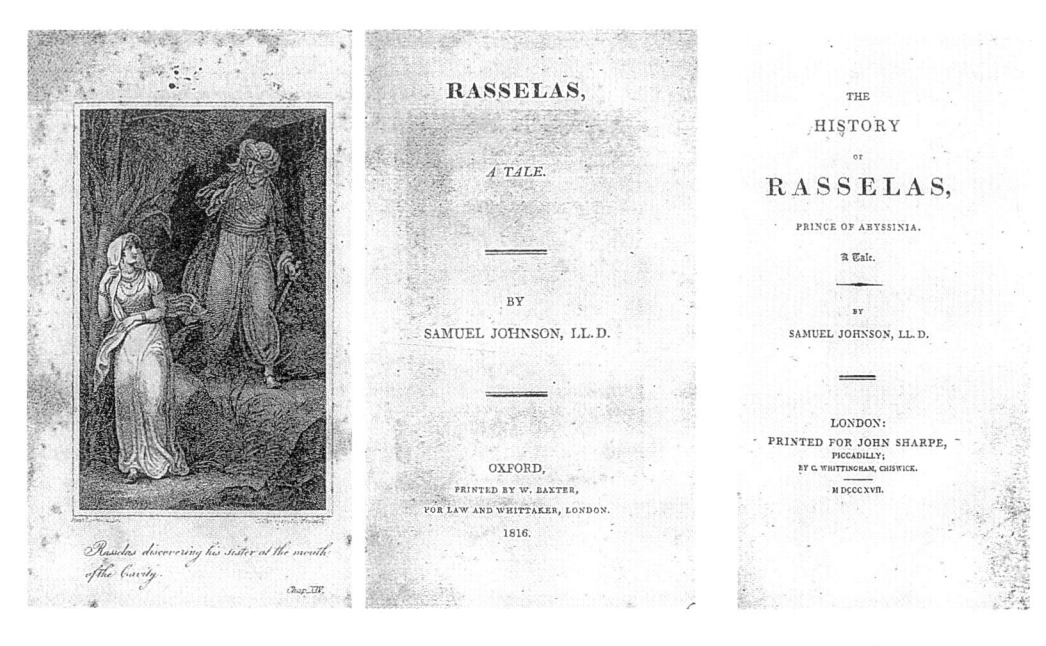

C−18 (1816) オックスフォード版

C−19 (1817)

RASSELAS,

BY

SAMUEL JOHNSON, LL.D.

WITH

ENGRAVINGS, BY A. RAIMBACH,

FROM

PICTURES BY R. SMIRKE, R.A.

LONDON:
PUBLISHED BY HECTOR M'LEAN, NO. 8, SOHO SQUARE;
AND SOLD BY MANNERS AND MILLER, AND ARCHIBALD CONSTABLE AND CO.
EDINBURGH.

1819

C − 20 (1819)

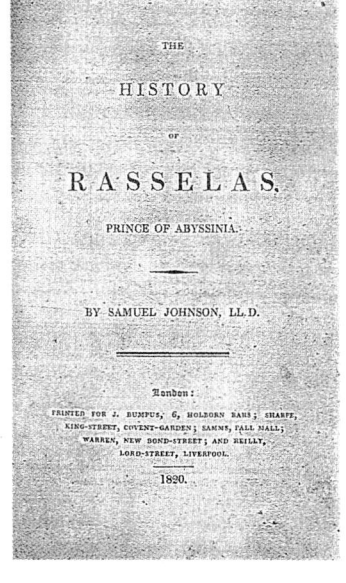

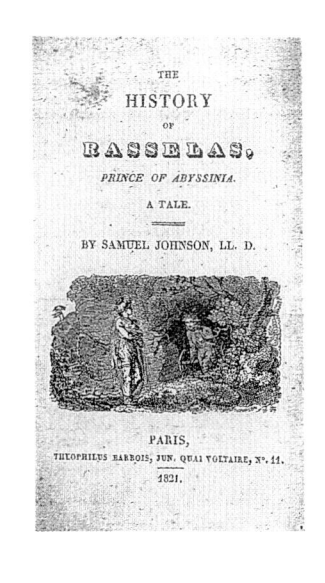

C − 21 (1820)

C − 22 (1821)

C−23 (1823)

C−24 (1823)   C−25 (1828)   C−26 (1835) ウエイトリィ作

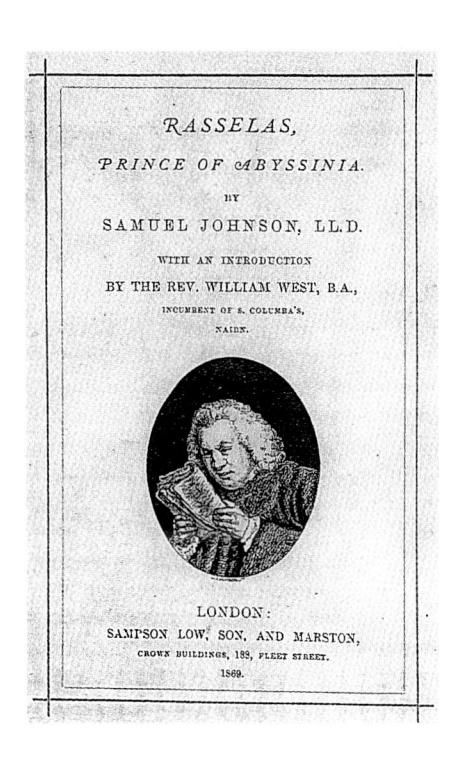

D—27 (1869)

D—28 (1884)

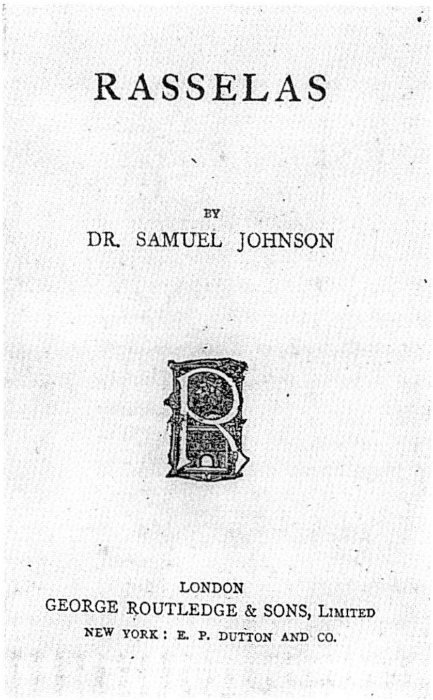

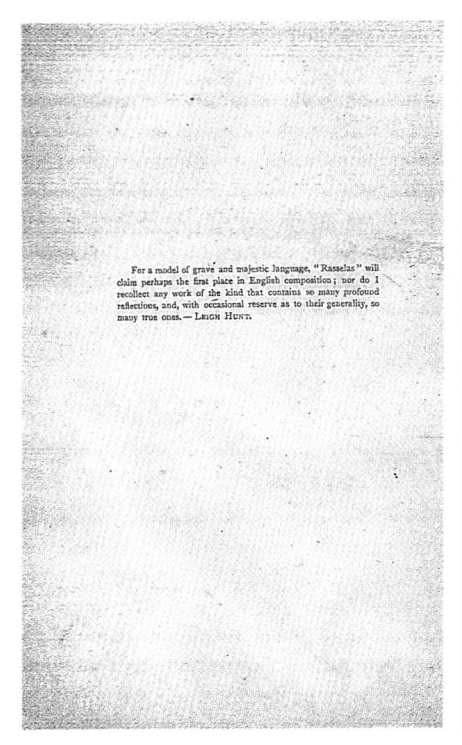

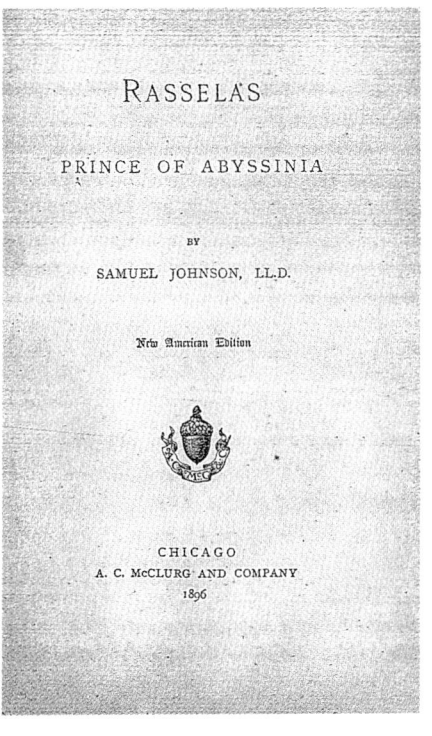

D—29 (1896) シカゴ版

E－30 (n.d.)   E－31 (n.d.)

『ラセラス』受容史の研究(2)

The Reception-History of *Rasselas*; In the Case of the Editions (2)

This paper is the second instalment of *The Reception-History of Rasselas; In the Case of the Editions* which was appeared in the *Memoirs*, vol.28, 1995. In this issue, approximately 25 items are introduced along with their illustrations. In section (A), 4 Japanese translation of *Rasselas* in the Meiji era are presented as the supplements to the editor's book, *Kentou no Bungou Johnson* (*Samuel Johnson in the Meiji Period*, 1992). In the second section (B), 6 works which have eluded the editor in the past are traced to complement the previous report. The next sections, (C), (D), and (E), deal with the popular editions of *Rasselas* which are easily accessible to modern readers. It should be made clear that in the present list that the editor has presented in the cursory manner, of course, too "much is omitted," so that it makes no claim to being exhaustive or comprehensive. Any reader who is interested in Samuel Johnson is requested to consult such a complete, up-to-date bibliography of Johnson as the Late Dr Fleeman's.

Keywords: Samuel Johnson, *Rasselas*, Meiji era, Editions, Translations, Works, Popular editions, Bibliography.

　本稿は，前稿「『ラセラス』受容史の研究」に続いて新たな『ラセラス』版本のご紹介である。無論，これらは完全なものでも，敢えて収集の労をとったものでもなく，ただ現在著者の身辺にあって，これまで触れることのなかった25冊について，補足として列挙したものである。最初に明治期のわが国において，出版された『ラセラス』版本の内，拙著『健闘の文豪ジョンソ

ン』(1992) において触れることのできなかったものについてご紹介し，次いで昨年の稿の補足として6冊をとり上げ，さらに普及版，合本版，翻訳版についてもご紹介しておいた。無論，これらが完璧なものでないことは言うまでもない。

I．はじめに

　ジョンソンの『ラセラス』(Samuel Johnson, *The History of Rasselas, Prince of Abyssinia*) は1759年に初版が刊行された後，おびただしい数の版本が流布し，時代と国境を越えて読まれてきたことはすでにご承知のとおりである。各種の書誌，蔵書目録が示すように，2・半世紀近くに及ぶ，その経緯は山間のささやかな流れが大河となって人心の沃地を潤す感がある。本稿では，現在筆者の身辺に置かれている約25冊の『ラセラス』本をご紹介し，さらなる展望の端緒としてみたい。Aでは，わが国において刊行された訳書，翻刻本の内，拙著『健闘の文豪ジョンソン — 明治期「ラセラス」の片影』(渓水社，平成4年) において，触れることのできなかった4冊について補足としてご紹介し，Bでは，前号でご紹介した18, 19世紀の版本に加えて，新たに入手した6冊，Cでは，現在比較的入手しやすい普及版7冊，Dでは，他書との合本版，訳本2冊，Eでは，これまで出版された『ジョンソン著作集』の一巻として刊行された『ラセラス』版6冊，合計25冊について検討してみたい。

II．明治期『ラセラス』の片影（補遺）

　明治時代においては，当初より英学は国威昂揚の極めて重要な担い手であった。これに呼応する英語教育は当初は舶載本によってなされ，英語熱の増大とともに翻刻本の流布，テキストの相次ぐ出版となって現れてきた。ジョンソンの『ラセラス』も明治15年頃から好読物の英語教科書として各社より出版されていたことが確認されている。A－1は1885（明治18）年出版の英語テキストであるが，その前年1884（明治17）年には東京大学文学部から同様の翻刻本が出版されていることから見て，東大では早くから『ラセラス』がテキストとして使用されていたことが分かる。荒正人著『漱石研究年表』（集英社，初版昭和49年，増補改訂版昭和59年）では，1903（明治36）年に，一高で『ラセラス』を教えたことが記述されている。（P.330）中勘助も「夏目先生と私」と題する随筆において，「私が一高の一年の時，……これまでの英語の先生が辞職してかわりの先生がくることになった。……それが夏目先生であった。……<u>教科書は前からのひき続きでじょんそんのらせらす</u>であった。」（同書，P.330，下線は筆者）と回顧している。「恐ろしく気取った — それだけ正確な — 発音のしかたで」，彼は学生たちの英語読解力の不足を，文学以前の問題として徹底的にたたきなおしたのである。A－2は新井清彦訳述の直訳附訳本であるが，これも英学生を対象として相当数売れたものと思われる。明治時代の『ラセラス』は年とともに，通俗的商品としても当時の出版界に歓迎されたのである。A－3は1912（大正元）年発行の斎藤秀三郎編纂の『ラセラス』本であるが，これをもって，さしものわが国における『ラセラス』熱も鎮静化してくることになる。A－4は，初版が1948年（昭和23）年9月に思索社から出版された後，吾妻書房から再発行されたものである。敗戦後の荒涼たる境遇の中での仕事であったことが訳者の「あとがき」から窺われる。

1．A－1（1885：明治18年）
　THE HISTORY OF RASSELAS, PRINCE OF ABYSSINIA. BY SAMUEL JOHNSON. / TOKIO: *TOKIO PUBLISHING COMPANY.*　2545, (1885).　東京同盟出版書肆／明治十八年三

月十三日出版御届／（ラセラス）／出版人　加藤鎮吉，石川貴知，岩藤錠太郎，江草斧太郎，大平俊章，亀井忠一

2．A－2（1894, 5：明治27, 8年）

　英国　如温遜氏原著／日本　新井清彦訳述　刺世拉斯氏釈義・直訳附　京都書肆　文港堂出版／明治二十七年二月十三日発行　同　二十八年四月十五日再版／著作者　新井泰之助／発行者　河合卯之助／印刷者　瀬戸清次郎

3．A－3（1912：大正元年）

　RASSELAS BY DR.SAMUEL JOHNSON EDITED BY H.SAITO ／ TOKYO: THE NICHI EISHA, 1912

4．A－4（1948, 62：昭和23, 37年）

　ジョンソン著／朱牟田夏雄訳　幸福の探求 ── アビシニアの王子ラセラスの物語 ──／吾妻書房刊／一九六二年九月二十日　初版発行

Ⅲ．『ラセラス』版（補遺）

　今日残されている数多い『ラセラス』版本の内，その後入手したために，前号で触れることのなかった6書を追加しておきたい。第3版（B－1）は前号（A－4, 1760）でも掲げているが，新たに第2巻も合わせた完本であるから，B－2（1798）の第10版とともにご紹介しておきたい。B－3（1805）の版も前号（C－13, 1805）でも触れているが，この豪華本に描かれている章頭の装飾図案（vignette）と4枚の彫版画も捨てがたいので，再度取り上げることにした。この版は1819年に出版者が変わって再版が出ている。B－5はCassell's Little Classicsのvol.9である。Collins編の『ラセラス』は紙表紙の小型の廉価本であって，詳細な序文（Introduction, pp.ix-xxix）と注解（Notes, pp.108-129）のある点からも，当時のイギリスにおける学徒，独学者向きの出版物であったことが分かる。初版の出版年は1910年であるが，この第3刷りの出版年月は不明である。

5．B－1（1760, Vol.Ⅰ, Ⅱ）3版

　THE PRINCE OF ABISSINIA. A TALE. IN TWO VOLUMES. VOL.Ⅰ. THE THIRD EDITION. ／ LONDON: Printed for R. and J. Dodsley, in Pall-Mall; and W. Johnston, in Ludgate-Street. MDCCLX.

6．B－2（1798）10版

　THE PRINCE OF ABISSINIA. A TALE. THE TENTH EDITION. LONDON: PRINTED FOR F. AND C. RIVINGTON, ／ T. N. LONGMAN, G. WILKIE, ／ J. WALKER, AND LEE AND ／ HURST. MDCCXCVIII.

7．B－3（1805）

　RASSELAS, BY ／ SAMUEL JOHNSON, LL.D. ／ WITH ENGRAVINGS, BY A. RAIMBACH, ／ FROM ／ PICTURES BY R. SMIRKE, R.A. ／ LONDON: PUBLISHED BY WILLIAM MILLER, ALBEMARLE-STREET; ／ AND SOLD BY MANNERS AND MILLER, AND ARCHIBALD CONSTABLE AND CO. ／ EDINBURGH. ／ The Letter Dress by James Ballantyne, Edinburgh. ／ 1805.

8．B－4（1887）

　JOHNSON ／ HISTORY OF RASSELAS ／ PRINCE OF ABYSSINIA ／ EDITED ／ *WITH INTRODUCTION AND NOTES* ／ BY GEORGE BIRKBECK HILL, D.C.L., LL.D. ／ HONORARY FELLOW OF PEMBROKE COLLEGE, ／ OXFORD AT THE CLARENDON PRESS

9. B－5 (1909)

RASSELAS / PRINCE OF ABYSSINIA / By / SAMUEL JOHNSON, LL.D. / With an Introduction by HENRY MORLEY / Cassell and Company, Limited / London, New York, Toronto and Melbourne / 1909

10. B－6 (1910)

JOHNSON / THE HISTORY OF RASSELAS / PRINCE OF ABYSSINIA / EDITED BY A. J. F. COLLINS, M.A. OXON. / EDITOR OF SHAKESPEARE: CORIOLANUS: HENRY Ⅳ. PARTS Ⅰ AND Ⅱ. HENRY V. / THIRD IMPRESSION / LONDON: W.B. CLIVE / UNIVERSITY TUTORIAL PRESS Ld. / HIGH ST., NEW OXFORD ST., W.C.

Ⅳ．普及版

ここでは第2次大戦後の比較的入手しやすい普及版について見てみた。C－1 (1959) とC－2 (1962) は『ラセラス』版ではないが，この物語の舞台となったエジプトのカイロの出版物であり，編者は著名なジョンソン学者である。C－5 (1975) はこの物語が今日においても，児童の夢と想像をかり立てる読み物であることが分かる。C－7 (1977) はインドのデサイ教授による詳細かつ適切な注解つきのテキスト版である。

11. C－1 (1959)

BICENTENARY ESSAYS / ON / *RASSELAS* / Collected by / MAGDI WAHBA / Supplement to / CAIRO STUDIES IN ENGLISH / 1959

12. C－2 (1962)

JOHNSONIAN STUDIES / including / A Bibliography of Johnsonian Studies, 1950-1960 / compiled by / James L. Clifford & Donald J. Greene / edited by / MAGDI WAHBA / CAIRO 1962

13. C－3 (1968)

THE WORLD'S CLASSICS / SAMUEL JOHNSON / *THE HISTORY OF RASSELAS / PRINCE OF ABISSINIA / Edited with an Introduction by* / J.P. Hardy / Oxford New York / OXFORD UNIVERSITY PRESS

14. C－4 (1971)

SAMUEL JOHNSON / THE HISTORY OF / RASSELAS / PRINCE OF ABISSINIA / Edited with an Introduction by / GEOFFREY TILLOTSON / and / BRIAN JENKINS / LONDON / OXFORD UNIVERSITY PRESS / NEW YORK TRONTO / 1971

15. C－5 (1975)

SAMUEL JOHNSON / The History of / RASSELAS / Prince of Abyssinia / With an Introduction by / Gilbert Phelps / and Lithographs by / Edward Bawden / LONDON / THE FOLIO SOCIETY / MCMLXXV

16. C－6 (1976)

SAMUEL JOHNSON / The History of Rasselas, / Prince of Abissinia / *Edited wih an introduction by* / *D.J. Enright* / PENGUIN BOOKS

17. C－7 (1977)

THE HISTORY OF / RASSELAS, / PRINCE OF ABYSSINIA / *BY* / SAMUEL JOHNSON / *Edited* / with an Introduction and Notes / *By* / R. W. DESSAI / DOABA HOUSE, DELHI

V. 合本版，訳本版

『ラセラス』はその類似性から外の物語との合本で出版されることがよくあった。前号（C-23, 1823）においても，『ディナバス』との合本版を紹介しておいたが，ここでは，Morley's Universal Library 19として出版されたヴォルテールの『カンディート』との合本のみ挙げておいた。無論，外にも次のような物語と合本で刊行されていることがボトレアン図書館『蔵書目録』は示している。

1. *The History of the Caliph Vathek*, by William Beckford [tr. by S. Henley], London, 1882, 3
2. *The Vicar of Wakefield*, by Oliver Goldsmith, London, 1883
3. *Almoran and Hamet*, by Dr. Hawkesworth, London, 1820

『ラセラス』の続編であるナイトの『ディナバス』は，今日においても合本で出版されている。

4. Samuel Johnson: *The History of Rasselas, Prince of Abyssinia* and Cornalia Knight: *Dinarbus*, Edited by Lynne Meloccaro, J.M. Dent: Vermont: Charles E. Tuttle, 1994

翻訳版は当初より，フランス語訳，ドイツ語訳，イタリア語訳，以下各国語訳が出されているが，未だ入手しえない故フリーマン先生の『書誌』（*Samuel Johnson Bibliography*, Oxford, 1996）では日本語訳としては合計13点が記載されているはずである。

18. D-1 (1884)

VOLTAIRE'S / CANDIDE OR THE OPTIMIST / AND / RASSELAS PRINCE OF ABYSSINIA / BY / SAMUEL JOHNSON / *WITH AN INTRODUCTION BY HENRY MORLEY* / LL.D,, PROFESSOR OF ENGLISH LITERATURE AT / UNIVERSITY COLLEGE, LONDON / LONDON / GEORGE ROUTLEDGE AND SONS / BROADWAY, LUDGATE HILL / NEW YORK: 9 LAFAYETTE PLACE / 1884

19. D-2 (1993)

Samuel Johnson / Histoire de Rasselas / prince d' Abyssinie / Introduction, traduction révisée et notes / par alain Montandon / ADOSA

VI. 著作集・選集

ジョンソンの『著作集』（Collected Works）や『選集』（Selections）に入れられた『ラセラス』版もその数は相当なものであるが，ここでは筆者の身辺にある6点のみを挙げておいた。

20. E-1 (1820)

THE / WORKS / OF / SAMUEL JOHNSON, LL. D. / A NEW EDITION, / IN TWELVE VOLUMES. / TO WHICH IS PREFIXED, / AN ESSAY ON HIS LIFE AND GENIUS, / BY ARTHUR MURPHY, ESQ. / VOL. III. / CONTAINING ADVENTURER AND RASSELAS. / LONDON: / PRINTED FOR G. WALKER, J. AKERMAN, E. EDWARDS, J. HARWOOD, W. ROBINSON / AND SONS, LIVERPOOL; E. THOMSON, MANCHESTER; J. NOBLE, HULL: / J. WILSON, BERWICK; W. WHYTE AND CO. EDINBURGH; AND R. GRIFFIN / AND CO. GLASGOW. / J. Haddon, Printer, Tabernacle Walk. / 1820

21. E-2 (1825)

THE / WORKS / OF / SAMUEL JOHNSON, LL.D. / VOLUME THE FIRST. / OXFORD. / PRINTED FOR WILLIAM PICKERING, LONDON; / AND TALBOYS AND WHEELER, OXFORD. / MDCCCXXV

22. E－3 (1832)

THE / WORKS / OF / SAMUEL JOHNSON LL.D. / WITH AN / ESSAY ON HIS LIFE AND GENIUS, / BY / ARTHUR MURPHY, ESQ / FIRST COMPLETE AMERICAN EDITION, / IN TWO VOLUMES. / VOL. I . / STEREOTYPE OF A. PELL & BROTHER. / NEW-YORK: / GEORGE DEARBORN, PUBLISHER, / JOHN-STREET. CORNER OF GOLD. / SOLD BY COLLINS AND HANNAY, NEW-YORK. -CARTER, HENDEE. AND CO., BOSTON. / AND JOHN GRIGG, PHILADELPHIA. / M, DCCC, XXXII.

23. E－4 (1903)

RASSELAS / PRINCE OF ABISSINIA / BY SAMUEL JOHNSON / PAFRAETS BOOK COMPANY / TROY NEW YORK

24. E－5 (1930, 67)

THE HISTORY OF RASSELAS / PRINCE OF ABYSSINIA / BY SAMUEL JOHNSON / in *Shorter Novels: Eighteenth Century* / Edited with an Introduction by Philip Henderson / Dent: London / Everyman's Library / Dutton: New York

25. E－6 (1990)

SAMUEL JOHNSON / Rasselas and Other Tales / *EDITED BY GWIN J. KOLB* / NEW HAVEN AND LONDON: YALE UNIVERSITY PRESS /1990

Ⅶ. SJ 書誌

S. ジョンソン（Samuel Johnson, 1709-1784）の書誌には，次のようなものがある。外にも大英博物館図書館，ボドレアン図書館，各有名大学付属図書館，ジョンソン協会関係機関，個人収集家，英米古書店のカタログによっても，それぞれの所蔵本を知ることができる。わが国においては，研究社（Johnson's *Dictionary*），関西大学（The Samuel Johnson Collection of Kansai University, 70 items, 209 vols），京都外国語大学付属図書館（See no.7 below）にそれぞれのジョンソン・コレクションがある。

1 . *A Bibliography of Samuel Johnson*, by W. Courtney and D.N.Smith, with *Johnsonian Bibliography: A Supplement to Courtney*, by R.W. Chapman, with the collaboration of A.T. Hazen. Oxford University Press, 1915; New Castle, Delware. U.S.A.: Oak Knoll Books, 1984

2 . James L. Clifford and Donald J. Greene, "A Bibliography of Johnsonian Studies, 1950-1960," in *Johnsonian Studies*, ed. Magdi Wahba, Cairo, U.A.R., 1962

3 . James L. Clifford and D. J. Greene, Samuel Johnson: *A Survey and Bibliography of Critical Studies*, Minneapolis: University of Minesota Press, 1970

4 . *The New Cambridge Bibliography of English Literature*,ed. George Watson, vol.2, 1660-1800, pp.1122-1174, 1971

5 . D.J. Greene and J.A. Vance, *A Bibliography of Johnsonian Studies 1970-1985*, University of Victoria (B.C., Canada), 1987

6 . Edward Tomarken, *"A Chronological Checklist of Rasselas Criticism 1759-1986,"* in *Johnson, Rasselas, and the Choice of Criticism*, The University Press of Kentucky, pp.194-201, 1989

7. Daisuke Nagashima, "A Catalogue of the Samuel Johnson Collection in the Library of Kyoto University of Foreign Studies," in *Essays in Honor of Professor Haruo Kozu: On the Occasion of His Retirement from Kansai University of Foreign Studies*, ed. by Daisuke Nagashima & Yoshitaka Mizutori, The Intercultural Research Institute, Kansai University of Foreign Studies, pp.143-162, 1990
8. John David Fleeman, *Samuel Johnson Bibliography,* Oxford University Press, 1996

謝　辞

最後になったが，本稿をまとめるに際しても，日頃多くの方々から資料や情報のご援助をいただいた。筆者はただおのれの部屋に安座して身辺を見渡したに過ぎない。以下に記す諸氏に心から謝意を表わしたい。

諏訪部　仁教授（中央大学），鶴見大学図書館，Late Dr John David Fleeman (Pembroke College, Oxford University), Mr David Parker (Samuel Johnson Society of London), Dr W. Nicholls (Samuel Johnson Birthplace Museum), Ms B. Gathergood (Dr. Johnson's House Trust), Mr N.H. Godsmark (Antiquarian Books, England)

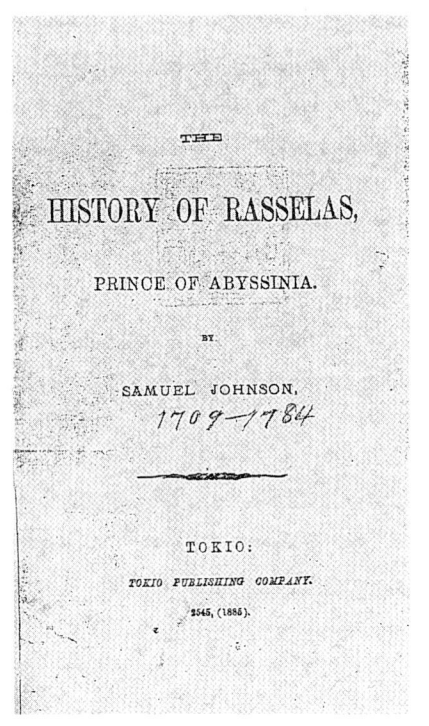

A－1(1885：明治18年)

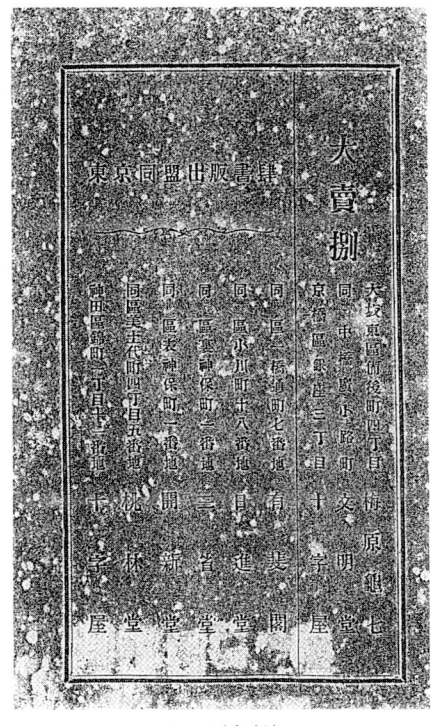

A－1(奥付)

A－1(奥付)

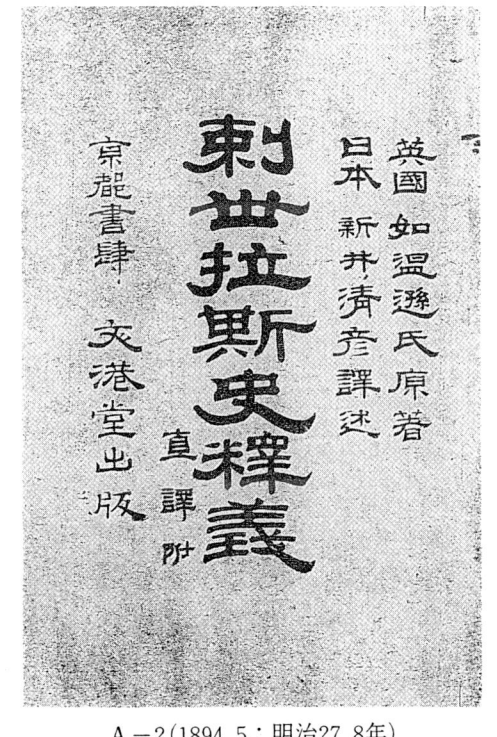

A－2(1894,5：明治27,8年)

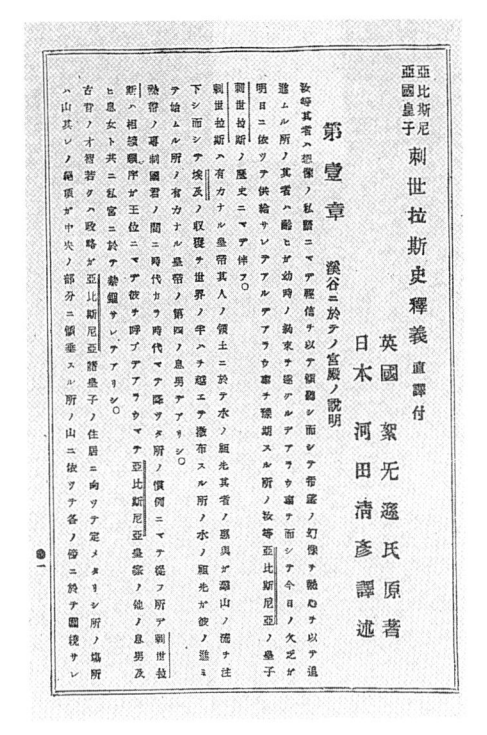

A−2（冒頭頁）

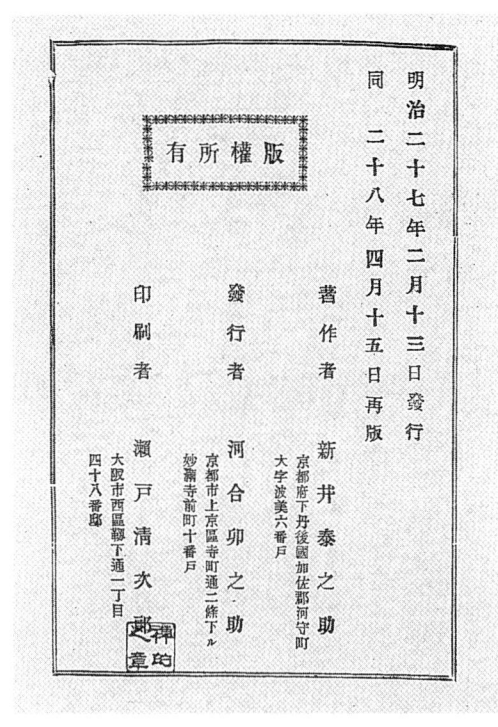

A−2（奥付）

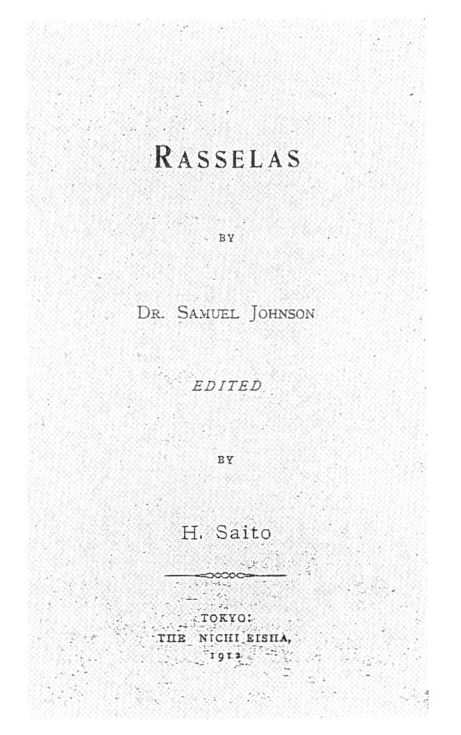

A−3（1912：大正元年）

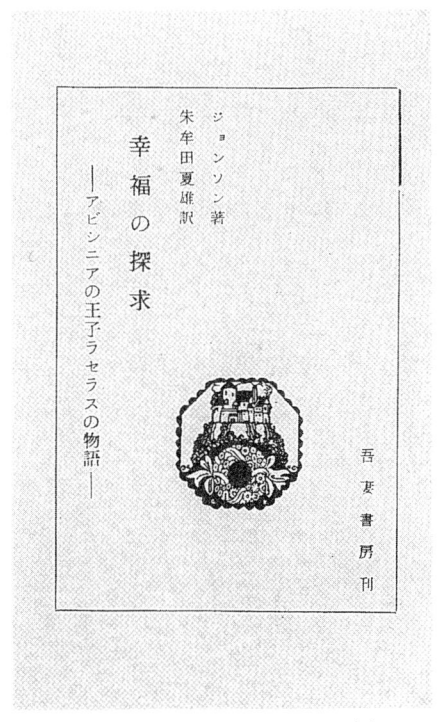

A−4（1948, 62：昭和23, 37年）

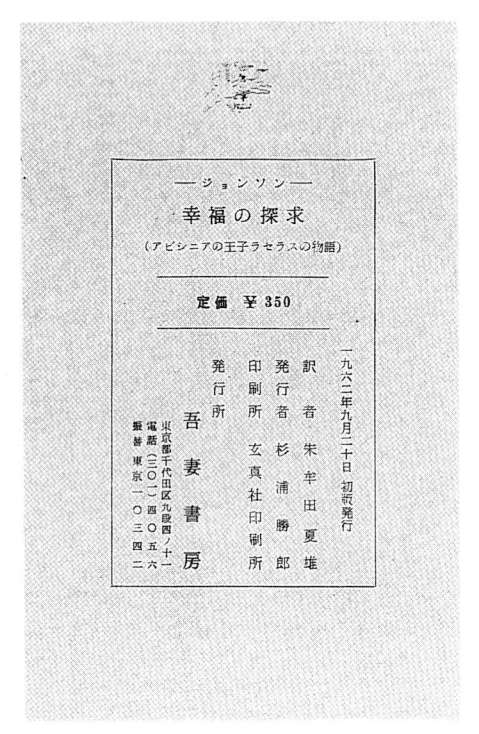

A−4(奥付)

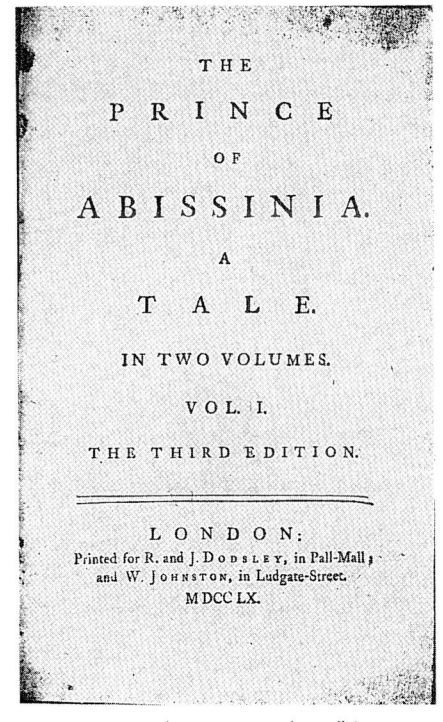

B−1(1760, Vol. I) 3版

B−1(Vol. II)

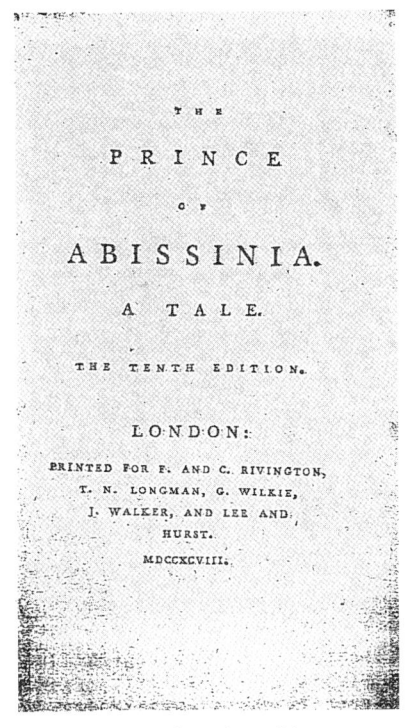

『ラセラス』受容史の研究(2)

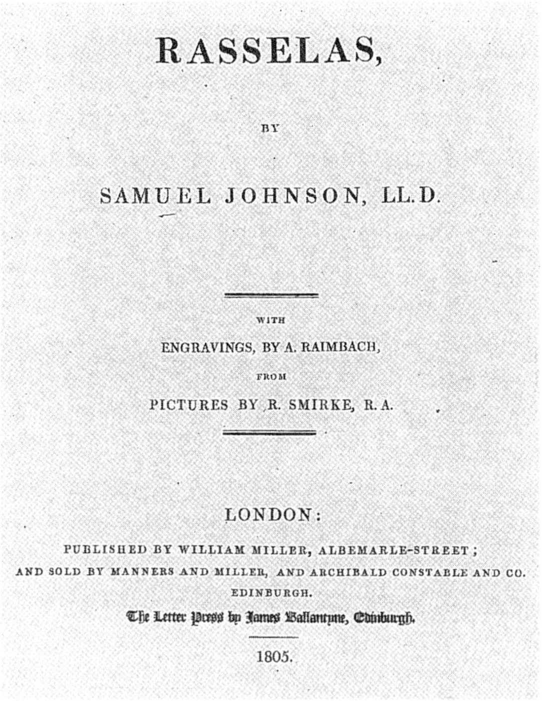

B−2(1798) 10版

B−3(1805)

B−3(ChAP. I)

B−3(ChAP. VI)

B-3(ChAP. XXI)

B-3(ChAP. XXXIII)

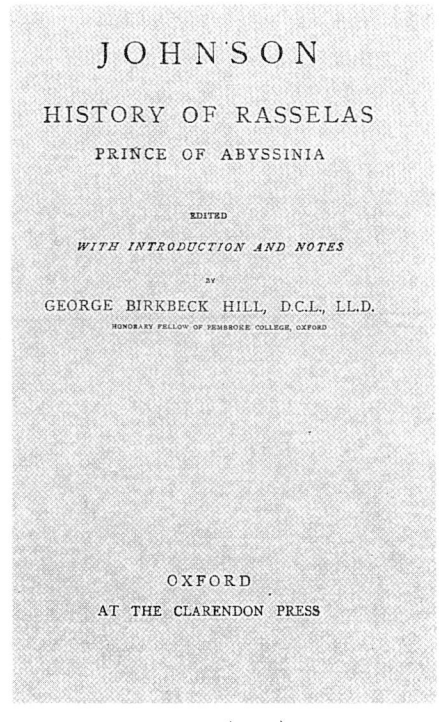

B-3(ChAP. XXXVIII)

B-4(1887)

B−5(1909)

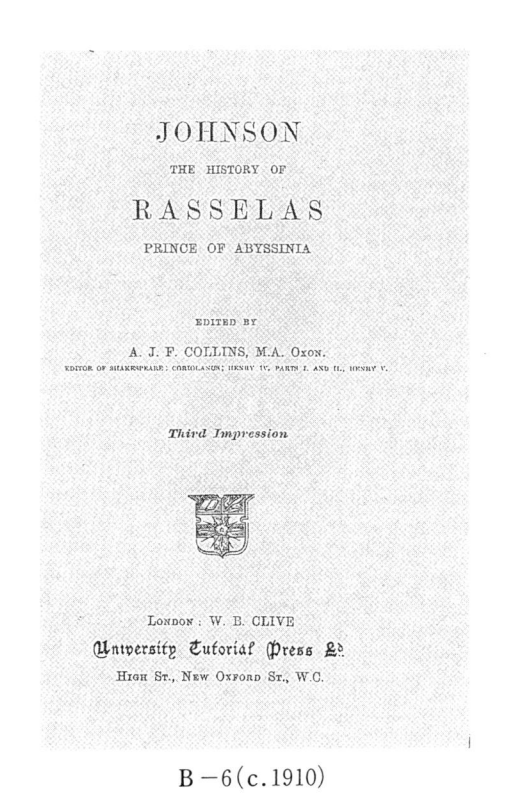

B−6(c.1910)

C−1(1959)

Chapter XXXV. Rasselas endeavoured first to comfort, and afterwards to divert her; he hired musicians, to whom she seemed to listen, but did not hear them…

C−1(CHAP. XXXV)

Chapter XLI. "… the sun has listened to my dictates…"

C−1(CHAP. XLI)

Chapter XVII. The consciousness that his sentiments were just, and his intentions kind, was scarcely sufficient to support him against the horror of derision.

C−1(CHAP. XVII)

Chapter XXIV. At last the letters of revocation arrived, the Bassa was carried in chains to Constantinople, and his name was mentioned no more.

C−1(CHAP. XXIV)

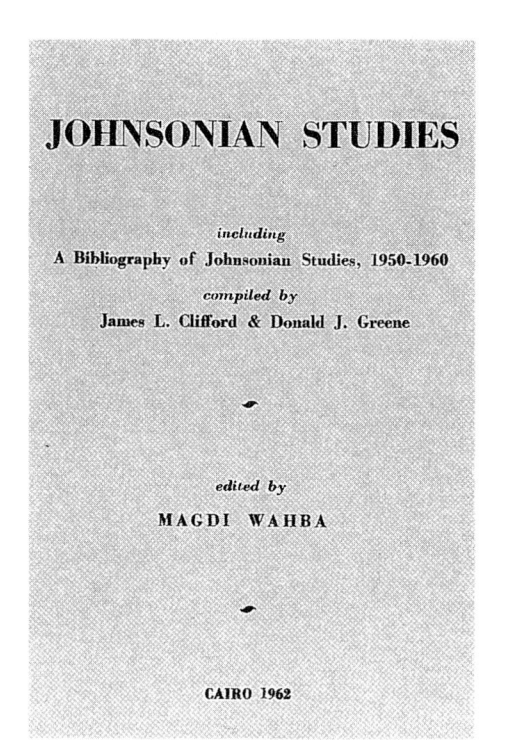

C−2(1962)

C−3(1968)

C−4(1971)

C−5(1975)

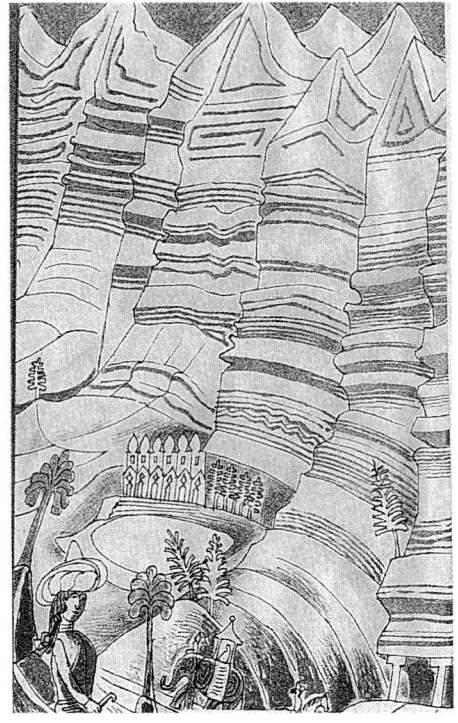

C-5(CHAP. I)

C-5(CHAP. III)

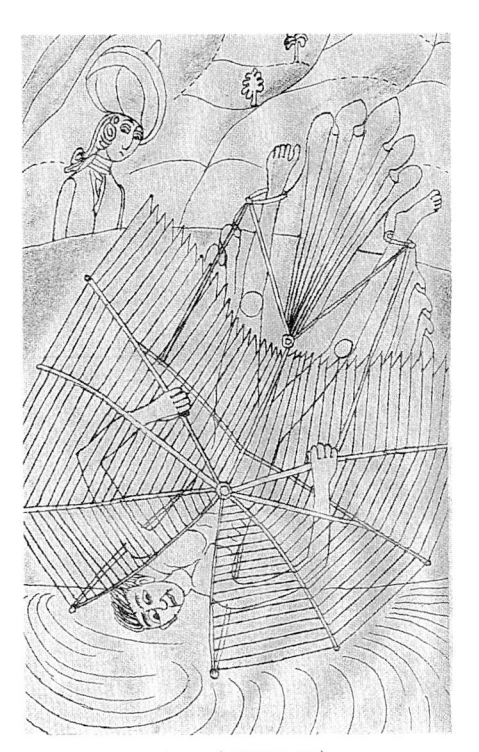

C-5(CHAP. VI)

C-5(CHAP. XIII)

『ラセラス』受容史の研究(2)

C−5(CHAP. XXII)

C−5(CHAP. XXXIV)

C−5(CHAP. XLVII)

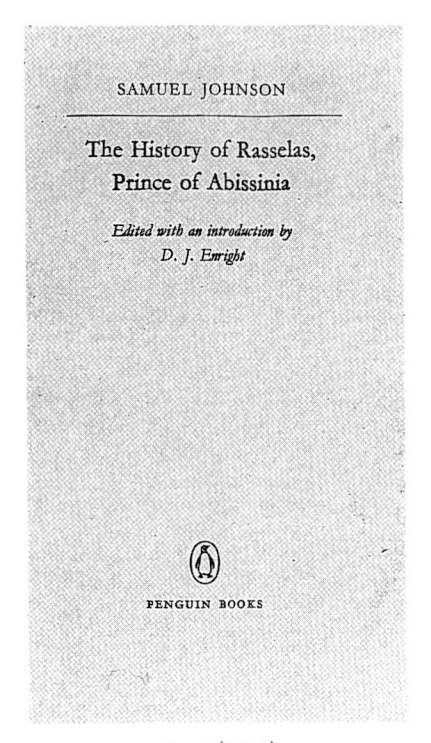

C−6(1976)

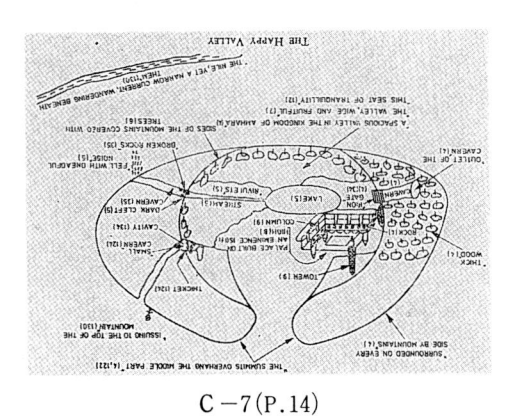

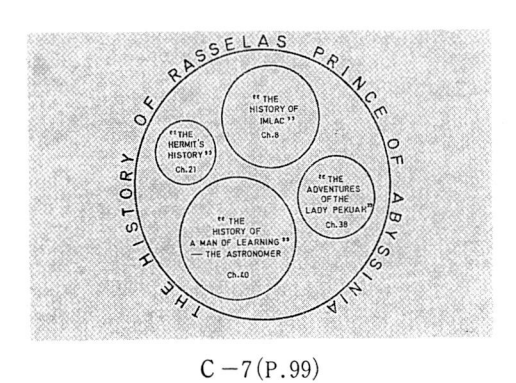

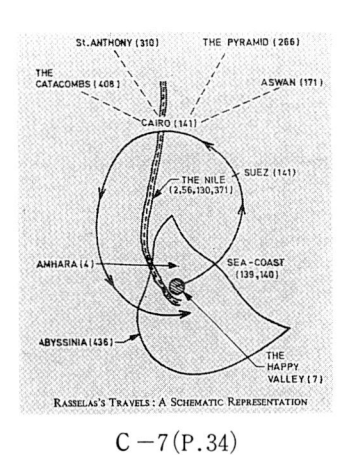

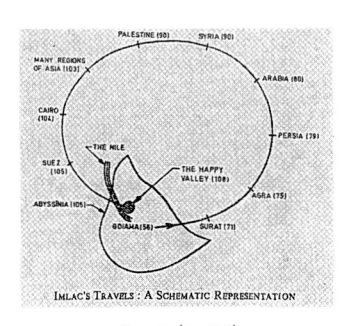

C−7(1977)

C−7(P.14)

C−7(P.34)

C−7(P.99)

C−7(P.67)

VOLTAIRE'S

CANDIDE OR THE OPTIMIST

AND

RASSELAS PRINCE OF ABYSSINIA

BY

SAMUEL JOHNSON

WITH AN INTRODUCTION BY HENRY MORLEY
LL.D., PROFESSOR OF ENGLISH LITERATURE AT
UNIVERSITY COLLEGE, LONDON

LONDON
GEORGE ROUTLEDGE AND SONS
BROADWAY, LUDGATE HILL
NEW YORK: 9 LAFAYETTE PLACE
1884

D−1(1884)

Samuel Johnson

Histoire de Rasselas
prince d'Abyssinie

Introduction, traduction révisée et notes
par Alain Montandon

ADOSA

D−2(1993)

THE
WORKS
OF
SAMUEL JOHNSON, LL.D.

A NEW EDITION,
IN TWELVE VOLUMES.

TO WHICH IS PREFIXED,

AN ESSAY ON HIS LIFE AND GENIUS,

BY ARTHUR MURPHY, ESQ.

VOL. III.

CONTAINING ADVENTURER AND RASSELAS.

LONDON:
PRINTED FOR G. WALKER, J. AKERMAN, E. EDWARDS, J. HARWOOD, W. ROBINSON
AND SONS, LIVERPOOL; E. TROMSON, MANCHESTER; J. NOBLE, HULL;
J. WILSON, BERWICK; W. WHYTE AND CO. EDINBURGH; AND R. GRIFFIN
AND CO. GLASGOW.
J. Haddon, Printer, Tabernacle Walk.
1820.

E−1(1820)

THE
HISTORY
OF
RASSELAS,
PRINCE OF ABISSINIA.

CHAP. I.
DESCRIPTION OF A PALACE IN A VALLEY.

YE who listen with credulity to the whispers of fancy, and pursue with eagerness the phantoms of hope; who expect that age will perform the promises of youth, and that the deficiencies of the present day will be supplied by the morrow; attend to the history of Rasselas prince of Abissinia.

Rasselas was the fourth son of the mighty emperor, in whose dominions the Father of Waters begins his course; whose bounty pours down the streams of plenty, and scatters over half the world the harvests of Egypt.

According to the custom which has descended from age to age among the monarchs of the torrid zone, Rasselas was confined in a private palace, with the other sons and daughters of Abissinian royalty, till the order of succession should call him to the throne.

The place, which the wisdom or policy of antiquity had destined for the residence of the Abissi-

E−1(CHAPTER I.)

E−2 (1825)

THE
WORKS
OF
SAMUEL JOHNSON, LL.D.

VOLUME THE FIRST.

OXFORD.
PRINTED FOR WILLIAM PICKERING, LONDON;
AND TALBOYS AND WHEELER, OXFORD.
MDCCCXXV.

E−2 (序論)

THE HISTORY
OF
RASSELAS, PRINCE OF ABISSINIA.

PREFATORY OBSERVATIONS.

The following incomparable tale was published in 1759; and the early familiarity with eastern manners, which Johnson derived from his translation of father Lobo's travels into Abissinia, may be presumed to have led him to fix his opening scene in that country; while Rassela Christos, the general of sultan Sequed, mentioned in that work, may have suggested the name of his speculative prince. Rasselas was written in the evenings of a single week, and sent to the press, in portions, with the amiable view of defraying the funeral expenses of the author's aged mother, and discharging her few remaining debts. The sum, however, which he received for it, does not seem large, to those who know its subsequent popularity. None of his works has been more widely circulated; and the admiration, which it has attracted, in almost every country of Europe, proves, that, with all its depression and sadness, it does utter a voice, that meets with an assenting answer in the hearts of all who have tried life, and found its emptiness. Johnson's view of our lot on earth was always gloomy, and the circumstances, under which Rasselas was composed, were calculated to add a deepened tinge of melancholy to its speculations on human folly, misery, or malignity. Many of the subjects discussed, are known to have been those which had agitated Johnson's mind. Among them is the question, whether the departed ever revisit the places that knew them on earth, and how far they may take an interest in the welfare

E−3 (1832)

THE
WORKS
OF
SAMUEL JOHNSON LL.D.

WITH AN
ESSAY ON HIS LIFE AND GENIUS,
BY
ARTHUR MURPHY, Esq.

FIRST COMPLETE AMERICAN EDITION,
IN TWO VOLUMES.
VOL. I.

NEW-YORK:
GEORGE DEARBORN, PUBLISHER,
JOHN-STREET, CORNER OF GOLD.

M.DCCC.XXXII.

E−3 (CHAPTER I)

RASSELAS.

CHAPTER I.
DESCRIPTION OF A PALACE IN A VALLEY.

Ye who listen with credulity to the whispers of fancy, and pursue with eagerness the phantoms of hope; who expect that age will perform the promises of youth, and that the deficiencies of the present day will be supplied by the morrow; attend to the history of Rasselas prince of Abissinia.

Rasselas was the fourth son of the mighty emperor, in whose dominions the father of waters begins his course; whose bounty pours down the streams of plenty, and scatters over the world the harvests of Egypt.

According to the custom which has descended from age to age among the monarchs of the torrid zone, Rasselas was confined in a private palace, with the other sons and daughters of Abissinian royalty, till the order of succession should call him to the throne.

E−4(1903)

E−5(1930,67)

E−6(1990)

『ラセラス』受容史の研究(3)

The Reception-History of *Rasselas*; In the Case of the Editions (3)

  This paper is the third instalment in the series of *The Reception-History of Rasselas: In the Case of the Editions*, part of the edition included in the *Memoirs*, of which the two have already appeared in the vols.28 (1995) and 29 (1996). In this survey, the focus is mainly on the editions and printings of / on Samuel Johnson and his *Rasselas* published in modern Japan. In the first section (A), which spans the time between 1868 (the Meiji Restoration) and 1911, thirty-four items are introduced with accompanying illustrated copy photographs. The second and third sections (B & C) are devoted to three books from the Taisho period (1912-1925), and eight books issued during the Showa period (1926-88). A brief glance at this chronological checklist reveals that it is practically impossible to trace all publications of the past to the editions concerning Samuel Johnson and his *Rasselas* because of the great difficulty in gaining access to them. The editor, however, expects that more than a few significant findings will be discovered in a future investigation.

Keywords：Samuel Johnson, *Rasselas*, Editions, Chronological checklist, Meiji period, Taisho period, Showa period.

  本稿は，一連の「『ラセラス』受容史の研究」の第3弾として，前号に続いて，さらなる『ラセラス』版本とその関連文献のご紹介である。本稿では，調査の対象を主として明治期におき，わが国における明治維新（1868）以後のジョンソンとその作品『ラセラス』の受容の経緯を批評史の視点からたど

って見たい。最初に，開国後出版されたおびただしい明治時代の和書の内より34冊，次いで大正時代の3冊，昭和時代の8冊をご紹介して見たい。今日，これらの収集は困難であるばかりでなく，調査のための閲読の機会を得ることさえも至難の業となっている。ここにご紹介した45冊の文献には，いずれもジョンソンに関わる言及，記事の見られるものである。無論，これらは完全なものでもなく，これまでに筆者の目に触れることのなかった興味深い発見が今後もあるものと思われる。

I. はじめに

わが国において英米の文学者やその作品が紹介導入されて，組織的に研究され，あるいは読まれてきた経緯は明治初期の激しい時勢の変遷や学制の改革とも密接に絡み合っている。お雇い外国人として当時東京大学の前身であった開成学校の英文学教師，James Summers，さらにその後任であった William A. Houghton は実にわが国の英米文学研究の端緒を築いた偉大な開拓者であった。わが国におけるションソンとその作品，とりわけ『ラセラス』の紹介とその普及の発端も実に彼等と，後にわが国の英学をリードすることになった二人の教え子たちの賜物であった。Samuel Johnsonの受容と流行の起源も彼等師弟がテキストとして，また参考文献として使用した書物の内に収められていたSJの抜粋文によることが既に判明している。しかし，これらの文献は散逸して筆者も未だ閲読することができない。一方広く世上の一般読書界に迎えられ，愛読された刊行物の内にも，ジョンソンの作品や伝記に関連した記事が多く見られる。本稿は明治開国以後出版された書物の内にジョンソンとその『ラセラス』に関連した版本，文献を年代順にご紹介したものである。(A)は明治時代，(B)は大正時代，(C)では昭和時代のものを掲げた。また，括弧内にそれらの記載箇所を示しておいた。アラビア数字は章，ページ番号を示している。SJはジョンソン関係，Rは『ラセラス』関係の記事のあることを示している。

II. 明治期 (1868, 明元〜1911, 明44)

明治時代を通して多大の影響を与えた敬宇中村正直の訳書はやはり冒頭に置かれなければならない。明治の青年たちの聖典であった彼の四大訳書にはSJへの言及記事が見られる。A−2 (千河岸) はA−1 (中村) に倣って，その後に出版された日本版であるが，刊行年月は不明である。A−9 (草野)，A−11 (田村)，A−12 (渡辺)，A−19 (大嶋)，A−26 (芝野)，A−33 (坂本) は『ラセラス』の翻訳版である。田村左衛士には，外に『アビシニアの王子ヨハネス伝』(1884, 明治14年)と言う興味深い訳書があるが筆者は未見である。A−13 (渋江)，A−16 (山田)，A−24 (坪内)，A−29 (栗原, 藤沢)，A−30 (浅野) 等の文学史，人名辞典には当然ながらSJとその作品の解説がある。A−21 (内田) はわが国最初の記念すべきSJの評伝であるが，A−4 (中村)，A−6 (尾崎)，A−7 (中原)，A−20 (大和田)，A−22 (井上) 中のSJ小伝もおもしろい。A−5 (橋爪) の「戒遜之伝」はSJではなく「ベンチャミン・ジョンソンノ伝」である。A−23にはマコーレーの学習書を1冊掲げておいたが，当時の英学習得の筆頭格であったことを示すためである。南洋田村左衛士も『泰西偉人』(1892, 明治25年9月) において，その第一にマコーレーを挙げているのである。A−28(松川)のホーソン訳は広くジョンソンの人柄を印象づけたものであり，明治41(1908)年，大日本図書株式会社発行の中等学校英語教科書にも転載されているものである。(See, *The Globe Reader*, Book Five, Arranged in Grades by Okakura Yoshisaburo, chaps 21-22, pp.81-90.）また，明治期の英語テキストとして，*The History of Rasselas, Prince of Abbyssinia / by Samuel Johnson* (Tokyo: Uhikaku, 1895; 123pp.19cm) が出版されたことも確認されている。未だ，入手していないが，当然拙著『健闘の文豪ジョンソン』（平成4年9月）の48-49頁に列記された「翻刻本の部」に追記されるべきものである。しかし，明治期を通して，真にSJとその『ラセラス』を理解し，本格的な論を展開したものはA-31（高橋）である。人生そのものに対して深い洞察力をもつ著者のSJ観を凌駕するものは今日まで出ていないように思われる。この書物は明治36年の初版以来既に17版を重ねていたベストセラーであった。

1．A-1（1870, 71：明治3, 4年）

　官許　明治庚午初冬新刻　中村正直訳／英国スマイルス著／西国立志編／原名　自助論／一千八百六十七年倫敦出版／SELF HELP. By Samuel Smiles. Translated by K.Nakamura.／駿河国静岡藩　木平謙一郎蔵版（第九編十一，第十編十，第十一編十四，外）

2．A-2（N.D.）

　干河岸貫一著／日本立志編　一名修身規範／板権所有　双書房合梓

3．A-3（1871：明治4年）

　一千八百七十年倫敦出版　英国　ミル著／ON LIBERTY BY JOHN STUART MILL／TRANSLATED BY K.NAKAMURA／SURUGA. 1871／明治辛未新刻　駿河静岡　中村敬太郎訳　木平謙一郎版，自由之理（第二巻十六）

4．A-4（1873：明治6年）

　一千八百七十二年　美国　ハルペル氏刊行／西国童子鑑／明治六年十月新刻／同人社　中村正直訳　木平譲梓（SJ．評論家，巻之三，一葉～七葉）

5．A-5（1879：明治12年）

　西国立志編列伝／明治十二年一月廿三日板権免許／訳者　橋爪貫一　出板人　木平愛二　外（十，B.J（ベンチャミン，ジョンソン）之伝）

6．A-6（1880：明治13年）

　尾崎行雄訳纂／泰西名家幼伝／明治十三年一月／明治十一年十二月三日版権免許／同十三年一月出版／訳纂出版人　尾崎行雄／発売書　慶応義塾出版社　外（SJ．評論家，下巻十一，二十七葉～三十三葉）

7．A-7（1880：明治13年）

　中洲三島先生閲　乾　立夫　中原淳蔵合訳／泰西名士鑑　上編全／東京書林　小泉堂発兌／明治十三年三月十日版権免許／同年十二月出版（SJ．自治之部，巻之七乃至巻之八）

8．A-8（1880：明治13年）

　亀谷省軒編／修身児訓／東京　光風社／明治十三年十一月廿五日版権免許／著書出版　東京府士族光風社長　亀谷　行（巻之二）

9．A-9（1886：明治19年）

　ジョンソン著　丈山居士訳／王子羅西拉斯伝記／明治十九年二月廿六日版権免許／同年三月刻成／翻訳兼出版人　熊本士族　草野　隆（明治19年2月，奎文堂）

10．A-10（1886：明治19年）

　西洋節用論目録（表紙欠）／明治十八年十二月十四日版権免許／同十九年二月出版／翻訳兼出板人　東京府士族　中村正直

11．A-11（1890：明治23年）

亜微志尼亜ノ王子　刺世拉斯伝／英国　如温遜原著／日本　峨洋逸人訳／明治廿三年四月十五日印刷／同年廿三年四月二十二日出版／訳述者　峨洋逸人　田村左衛士

12. A－12（1890：明治23年）
亜比斯尼亜国王子　刺西拉斯経歴史目録／明治二十三年十月廿四日　印刷／明治二十三年十月廿八日　出版／著作者　渡辺松茂／積善館

13. A－13（1891：明治24年）
渋江　保　編／英国文学史　全／東京　博文館蔵版（SJ.178～180）

14. A－14（1892：明治25年）
泰西名言　石村貞一著述　全／明治二十五年二月一日　再版印刷出版／著述者　山口士族　石村貞一／全国書肆（SJ.6，11，12）

15. A－15（1892：明治25年）
国民英学会主幹　磯部弥一郎講述／英文学講義録　第三巻／東京　国民英学会蔵版／明治二十五年九月廿二日印刷／同年同月廿三日出版（3巻："A Letter to Chesterfield"）

16. A－16（1893：明治26年）
山田武太郎編著／西洋及漢士之部／万国人名辞書　上巻／東京　博文館蔵版／明治二十六年七月七日印刷／明治二十六年七月十日発行（SJ.352～353）

17. A－17（1893：明治26年）
日本英学新誌　第三十七号／増田藤之助「ラセラス」伝の評／明治二十六年十月（R.1号～36号）

18. A－18（1893：明治26年）
日本英学新誌　第四十号／増田藤之助「ラセラス」の文章／明治二十六年十一月（3：433～435）

19. A－19（1893：明治26年）
日本　大島国千代著／ジョンソン氏ラセラス伝註釈／東京　金刺氏発兌

20. A－20（1894：明治27）
国民文庫第九編／大和田建樹著／英米文人伝　全／東京　博文館版（SJ.13：71～78）

21. A－21（1894：明治27年）
十二文豪　号外　ジョンソン　内田　貢著／明治二十七年七月十二日印刷／明治二十七年七月十五日発行／発行所　民友社

22. A－22（1897：明治30年）
大文豪／編集兼発行者　井上藤吉／明治三十年九月二十六日印刷／同三十年十月一日発行／発兌元　文錦堂書店（SJ.50～55）

23. A－23（1900：明治33年）
第七版　LORD CLIVE／BY／MACAURAY／高等英語通信会講／クライブ伝講義／東京　開新堂発兌

24. A－24（1901：明治34年）
文学博士　坪内　雄蔵著／文学叢書　英文学史／東京専門学校出版部蔵版（SJ.第4編 12：501～511）

25. A－25（1902：明治35年）
川上峨山著／恋愛の文豪／文学同志会蔵版（SJ.125～158）

26. A－26（1905：明治38年）
THE HISTORY OF RASSELAS／PRINCE OF ABYSSINIA／by DR.SAMUEL JOHNSON／

Translated and Annotated ／by／SHIBANO ROKUSUKE／with INTRODUCTION by UEDA BIN／明治三十八年六月十七日印刷／明治三十八年十月十日再版発行／校閲者　文学士　上田敏／訳述者　芝野六助／発兌大日本図書株式会社

27．A－27（1906：明治39年）

　The Lake English Classics／MACAULAY'S ESSAYS／ON ADDISON AND JOHNSON／EDITED FOR SCHOOL USE／BY ALPHONSO G. NEWCOMER／ASSOCIATE PROFESSOR OF ENGLISH IN THE LELAND STANFORD／JUNIOR UNIVERSITY／CHICAGO／SCOTT, FORESMAN AND COMPANY／1906

28．A－28（1907：明治40年）

　Bioraphical Stories／五偉人の少時／ナサニエル，ホーソン著／松川渓南訳（SJ．3：8：2～100）

29．A－29（1907：明治40年）

　文学士栗原　基　文学士藤沢周次共編／英国文学史／東京　博文蔵版／明治四十年二月五日印刷／明治四十年二月拾日発行（SJ．第6編3：182～185）

30．A－30（1907：明治40年）

　文学士浅野和三郎著／英文学史／付録　米国文学史／英詩之種類及韻律法／大日本図書株式会社／明治四十年二月廿五日印刷／明治四十年二月廿八日発行（SJ．第9編1：362～369，R．365）

31．A－31（1907：明治40年）

　高橋五郎著／増訂　人生観／東京　文栄閣蔵版／明治四十年五月十日印刷／明治四十年五月十五日発行（初版明治36年，17版，SJ．第2編59～63；R．46～64）

32．A－32（1908：明治41年）

　人生と健闘　田村逆水著／博文蔵版，明治41年1月29日発行（SJ．第1編16：153～162）

33．A－33（1909：明治42年）

　博士ジョンソン原著／坂本大風訳編／ラセラス王子物語／東京　内外出版会／明治四十二年十二月一日印刷／明治四十二十二月五日発行／著作者　坂本栄吉（R．88～96）

34．A－34（1911：明治44年）

　スヰントン氏／英文学詳解／全／岡村愛蔵訳註／NOTES／ON／STUDIES IN ENGLISH LITERATURE／BEING／TEPICAL SELECTIONS ON BRITISH ABD AMERICAN AUTHORSHIP, FROM SHAKESPEARE TO THE PRESENT TEIME／BY WILLIAM SWINTON／AUTHOR OF／"HARPER'S LANGUAGE SERIES" AND GOLD METALLIST〔sic〕／PARIS EXPOSITION 1878／EDITED BY AIZO P. OKAMURA／第5版／KOBUNSHA, TOKYO／1911（前編11；313～336）

Ⅲ．大正期（1912，大1～1925，大14）

　大正時代はわずか3冊のみ掲げた。B－1（山路）には短文ながら，一項目を設けてSJの略歴を詳解している。B－2はアメリカにおける学生向けのテキストか推薦図書版であり，かの地においても，マコーレーの影響は長く続いていたことが分かる。

35．B－1（1916：大正5年）

　山路愛山著／東西六千年／東京　春陽堂発行／大正五年二月二十日印刷／大正五年二月廿五日再版／著作者　山路弥吉（SJ．288～290）

36. B-2 (1922：大正11年)

MACAULAY'S／LIFE of SAMUEL JOHNSON／EDITED WITH NOTES AND AN INTRODUCTION／BY／WILLIAM SCHUYLER, A.M.／PRINCIPAL OF THE MCKINLEY HIGH SCHOOL／S.T.LOUS, MO,／NEW YORK／THE MACMILLIAN COMPANY／LONDON: MACMILLAN & CO.,LTD.／1922／All rights reserved（SJ. 170〜230, R. 200〜202）

37. B-3 (1924：大正13年)

広島文理科大学教授　小日向定次郎著／英文学史　ドライデン時代よりヴィクトリア王朝初期迄／文献書院発行／大正十三年十月二十二日印刷／大正十三年十月二十五日発行（SJ. 第3編4：307〜322；R. 318）

Ⅳ. 昭和期（1926, 昭1〜1988, 昭63）

この時代については正確な列挙は控えた。C-2（石田）は記念すべき大著であり，SJ への関心が高まったのもこの時期であった。筆者は未見であるが，昭和13年になっても，小松武治編のテキスト版『ラッセラス』（奥付標題）が出版されている。(*Rasselas. Prince of abyssinia*／by Samuel Johnson; compiled by T.Komatsu (Tokyo: Daito Press, 1938: 173pp. 19cm.) SJ に限らず，英学全般に対する史的研究も数多くの業績を生み出している。戦後は SJ 研究書も暇なく刊行されており，入手もまた比較的に容易である。

38. C-1 (1931：昭和6年)

Kenkyusya English Classics／THE LIFE OF／SAMUEL JOHNSON, LL.D.／BY／JAMES BOSWELL／SERECTED／WITH INTRODUCTION AND NOTES／BY／HARUJI OGURA／PROFESSOR OF ENGLISH IN THE FIRST HIGH SCHOOL／TOKYO／KENKYUSYA／1931.

39. C-2 (1933：昭和8年)

ジョンソン博士／と／その群／石田憲次著／東京　研究社　出版（SJ. 2：45〜248；R. 152〜164）

40. C-3 (1933：昭和8年)

サムエル・ジョンソン博士著／日本　鈴木二郎訳／祈祷と黙想／一粒社刊行／昭和八年六月十五日印刷／昭和八年六月二十日第一刷発行

41. C-4 (1934：昭和9年)

SAMUEL JOHNSON／by／KENJI ISHIDA／AND／JIRO SUZUKI／TOKYO／KENKYUSHA／1934／研究社英米文学評伝叢書 ―24―ヂョンスン／昭和九年三月十五日印刷／昭和九年三月二十日発行（R. 78〜79）

42. C-5 (1934：昭和9年)

金子健二著／東洋思想の西漸と英吉利文学／昭和九年三月三十一日印刷／昭和九年四月十日発行／印刷者　西川喜右衛門（SJ. 3：213〜218；R. 215）

43. C-6 (1935：昭和10年)

Boswell's Life of Johnson／Selected and Annotated／by／Shun Katayama／Professor of English in the Osaka University of Commerce／HIRANO SHOTEN／Kyoto (157pp.)

44. C-7 (1941：昭和16年)

岩波文庫　サミュエル・ヂョンソン伝／上／ボズウェル著／神吉三郎訳　岩波書店／昭和十六年六月二十日印刷／昭和十六年六月二十八日発行

45. C－8 （1972：昭和47年.）

　新英米文学評伝叢書／SAMUEL JOHNSON／福原麟太郎／1972／東京　研究社出版／昭和47年1月19日評伝印刷／昭和47年1月20日発行（R.19：221～233）

V. おわりに

　冒頭に指摘したように，わが国におけるSJ受容の発端は，本邦最初に英文学を講義した東京開成学校教師James Summers（1828－91）とその後任者であったWilliam A.Houghton（1852－1817）であった。彼らがテキスト，あるいは参考書として使用した下記の書物の内にSJ移入の起源があるものと考えられる。これらの文献の探索，検討が今後の課題である。（重久篤太郎『日本近世英学史』増補版，名著普及会，昭和57年11月，pp.315－389参照。）

> Underwood, Francis Henry (1825-94), *A Hand-book of English Literature*: Intended for the Use of High Schools, as well as a Companion and Guide for Private Students, and for General Readers, 2 vols, Vol.1.　British Authors; Vol.2, American Authors, Boston: Lee and Shepard, 1871-1872.
>
> Craik, George Lillie (1798-1866), *Compendious History of English Literature of the English Language* (1861) & *A Manual of the History of English Literature and the History of English Language*.
>
> Sprague, Homer Baxter (1829-1918), *Masterpieces in English Literature*.

　また，今日のわが国においては，ジョンソンとその作品，とりわけ『ラセラス』が広く大学，学会レベルにおいて，話題を呼ぶ程に取り上げられることも少なくなったが，アメリカにおいては，今日もなお，『ラセラス』は文学史や西欧思想史の概論（（The Introductory Course）でも必読のテキストとして，多くの大学において読まれていることも付記しておきたい。（See David R.Anderson & Gwin J.Kolb, eds., *Approaches to Teaching Samuel Johnson*〔New York: The Modern Language Association of America, 1993, pp.xi, 3,4,64-70, 121-27.〕）

官許 明治庚午初冬新刻

SELF HELP.
By Samuel Smiles.
Translated by M. Nakamura.

英國 斯邁爾斯 著
中村正直 譯

西國立志編
原名 自助論

一千八百六十七年倫敦出版

駿河國靜岡藩
木平謙一郎藏版

西國立志編 原名 自助論 第四冊

A－1（1870, 71：明治3，4年）

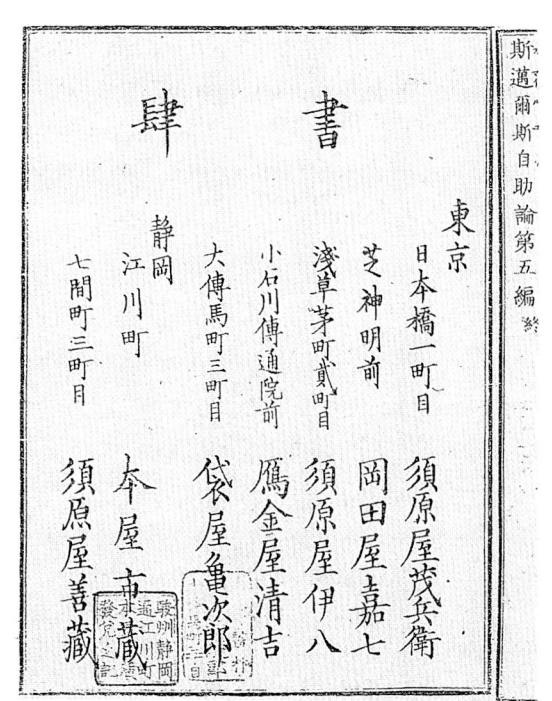

斯邁爾斯自助論第十三編

六書房藏版

小石川區江戸川町十七番地　木平愛二
神田區鍛冶町十二番地　高橋金十郎
日本橋區通三丁目十九番地　稻田佐兵衞
同區同町十八番地　稻田源吉
小石川區大門町廿五番地　青山清吉
神田區通新石町廿一番地　福田仙藏

斯邁爾斯自助論第五編終

東京
日本橋一町目　須原屋茂兵衞
芝神明前　岡田屋嘉七
淺草茅町貳丁目　須原屋伊八
小石川傳通院前　鷹金屋清吉
大傳馬町三丁目　袋屋龜次郎

靜岡
江川町　本屋市藏
七間町三町目　須原屋善藏

A－1（奧付）

A−2 (N.D.)

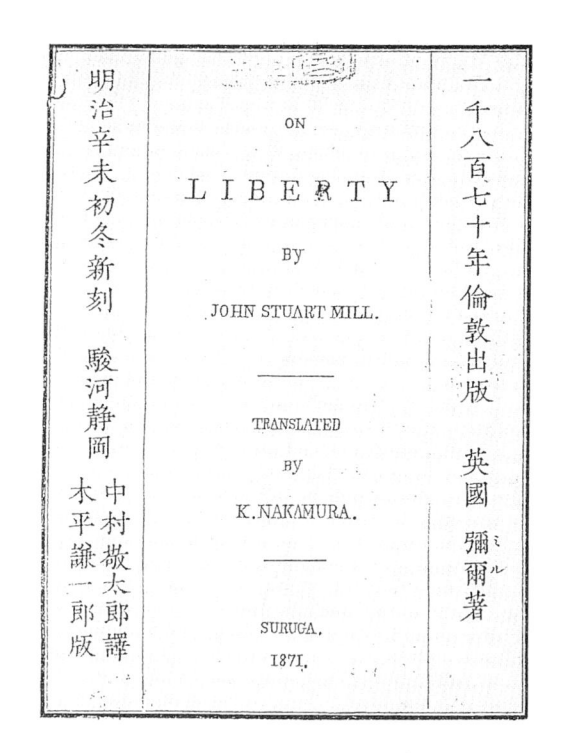

A−3 (1871：明治4年)

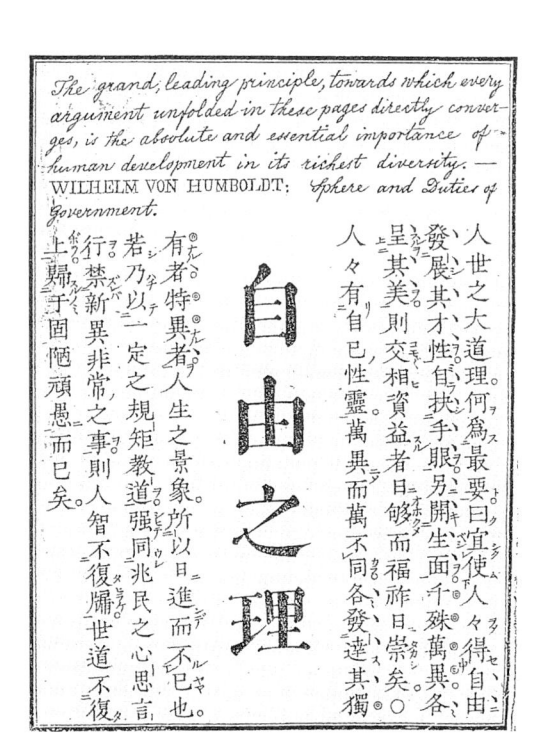

A−3 (扉)

A−4 (1873：明治6年)

A－5（1879：明治12年）

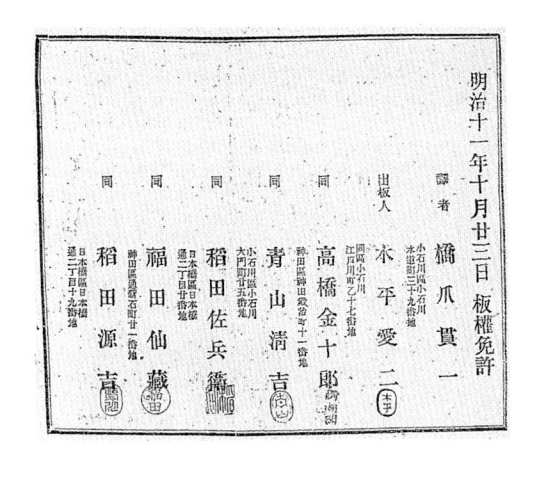

A－5（奥付）

A－6（1880：明治13年）

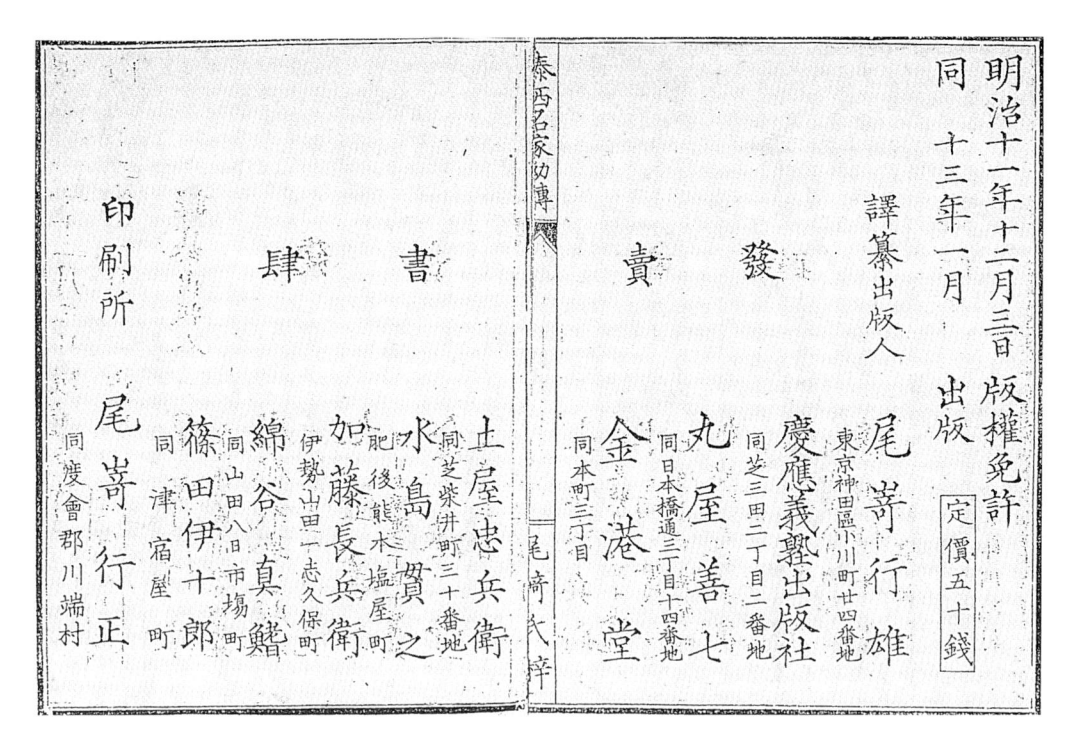

A-6（奥付）

A-7（1880：明治13年）

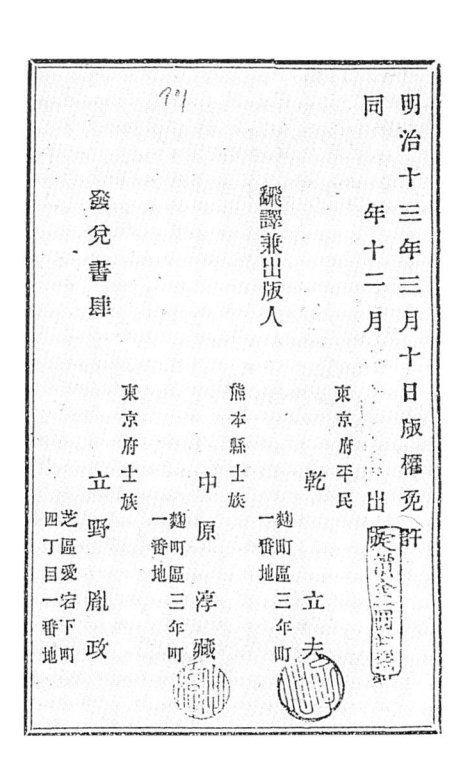

A-7（奥付）

A－8（1880：明治13年）

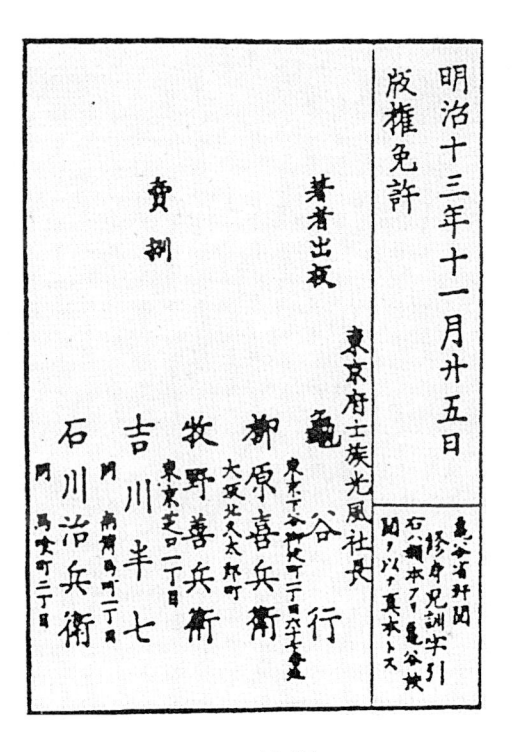

A－8（奥付）

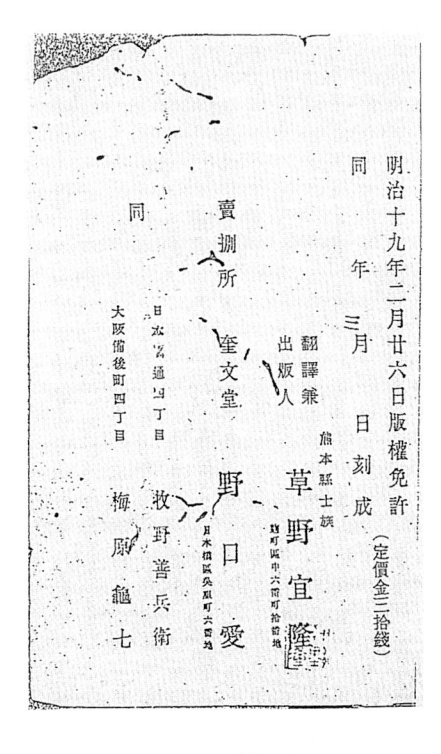

A－9（1886：明治19年）

A－9（奥付）

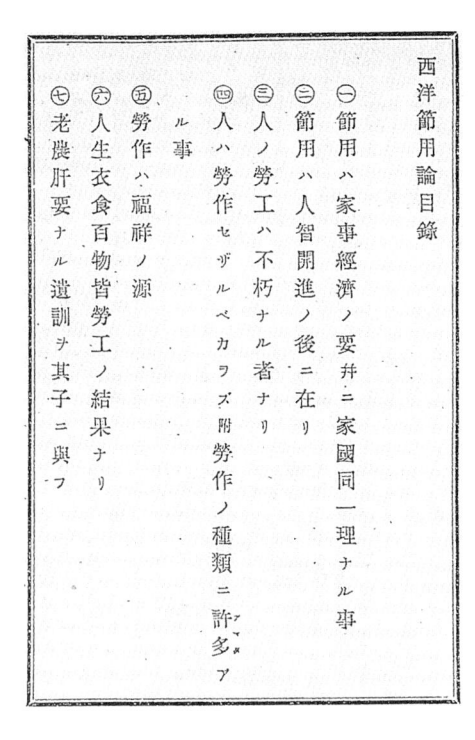

『ラセラス』受容史の研究(3)

西洋節用論目録

一　節用ハ家事經濟ノ要并ニ家國同一理ナル事
二　節用ハ人智開進ノ後ニ在リ
三　人ノ勞工ハ不朽ナル者ナリ
四　人ハ勞作セザルベカラズ附勞作ノ種類ニ許多アル事
五　勞作ハ福祥ノ源ナリ
六　人生衣食百物皆勞工ノ結果ナリ
七　老農肝要ナル遺訓ヲ其子ニ與フ

A-10（1886：明治19年）

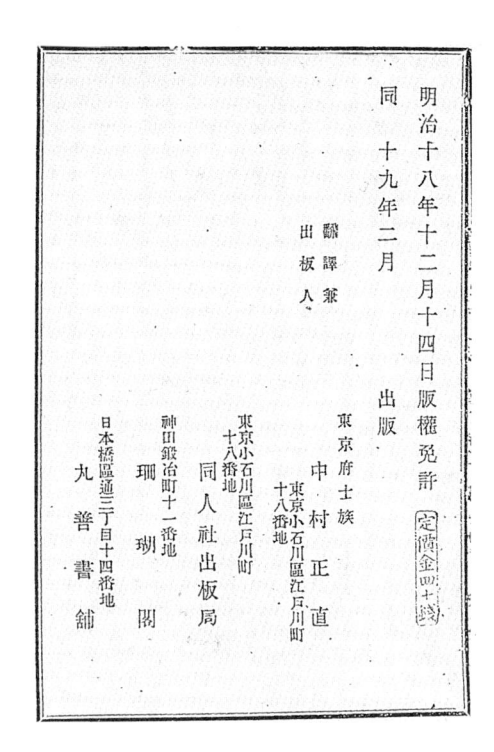

明治十八年十二月十四日版權免許　定價金四十錢
同　十九年二月　出版

翻譯兼出板人

東京府士族
中村　正直
東京小石川區江戸川町十八番地

同人社出板局
神田鍛冶町十一番地
珊　瑚　閣

日本橋通三丁目十四番地
丸　善　書　舗

A-10（奥付）

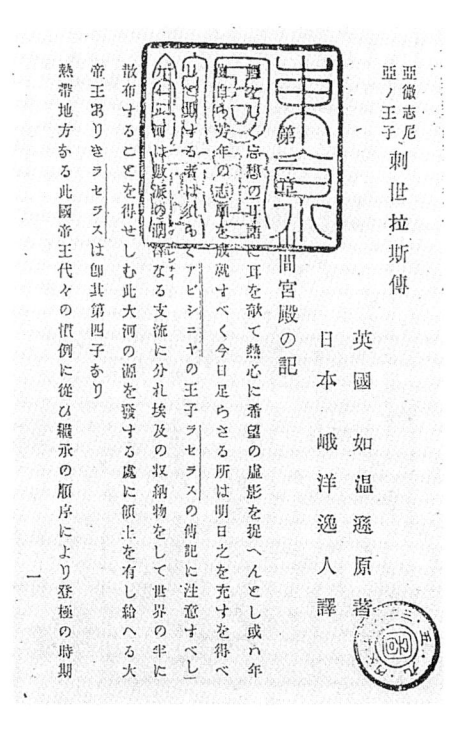

亞徹志尼
亞ノ王子刺世拉斯傳

英國　如温遜原著
日本　峨洋逸人譯

間宮殿の記

帝王出りきラセラスは即ち其第四子あり…（本文）

A-11（1890：明治23年）

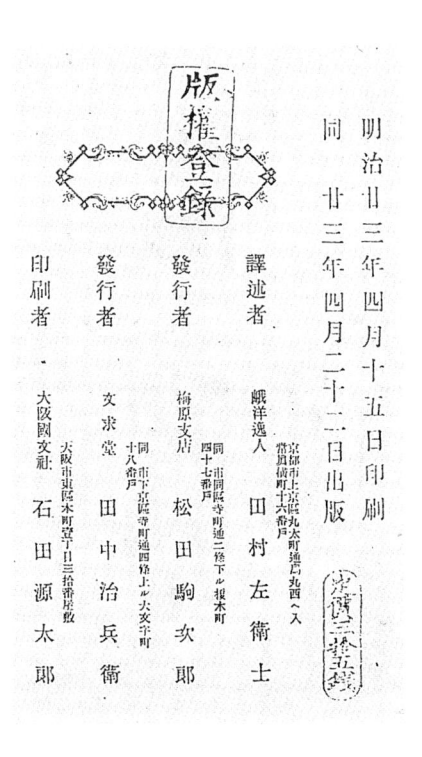

明治廿三年四月十五日印刷
同　廿三年四月二十二日出版

版權登錄

譯述者
嵯洋逸人　田村左衛士
京都市上京區丸太町通富丸西ヘ入

發行者
梅原支店　松田駒次郎

發賣所
文求堂　田中治兵衛
大阪市東區本町壹丁目三拾番屋敷

印刷者
大阪圖文社　石田源太郎

A-11（奥付）

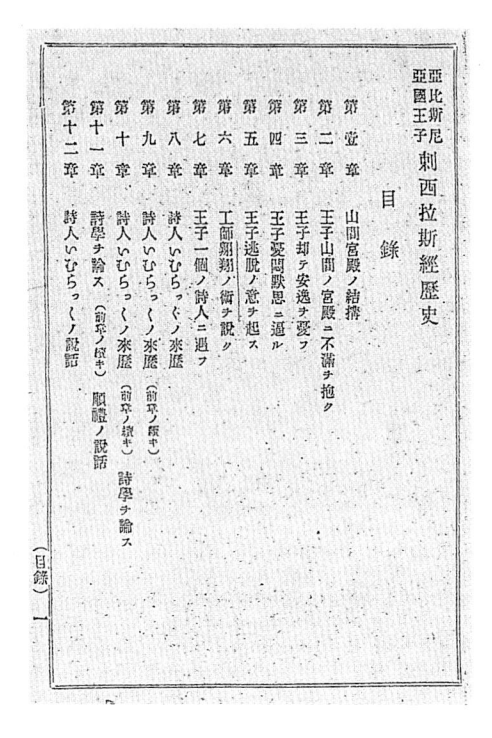

A-12 (1890：明治23年)   A-12 （奥付）

A-13 (1891：明治24年)   A-13 （奥付）

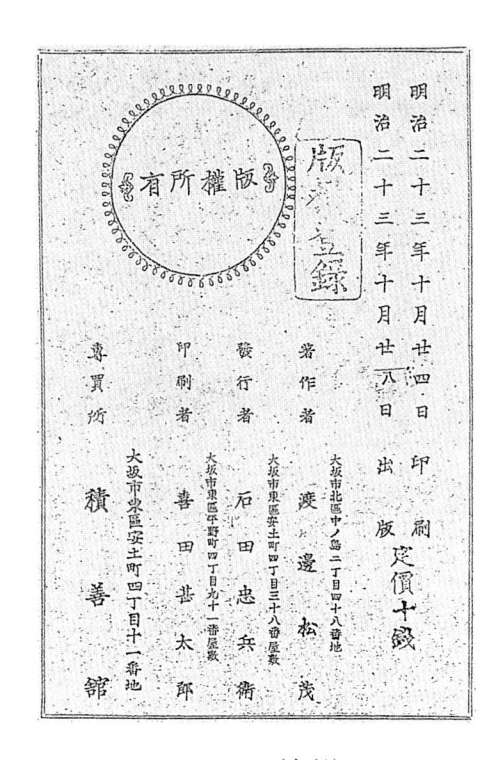

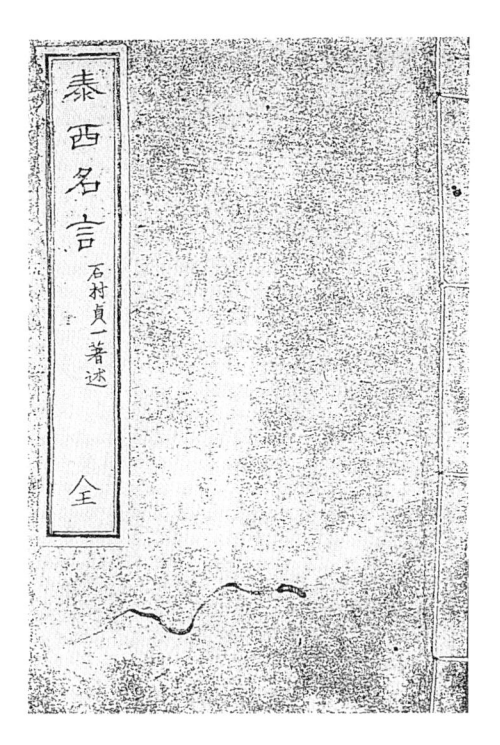

A－14（1892：明治25年）　　　　　　　　A－14（奥付）

A－15（1892：明治25年）　　　　　　　　A－15（奥付）

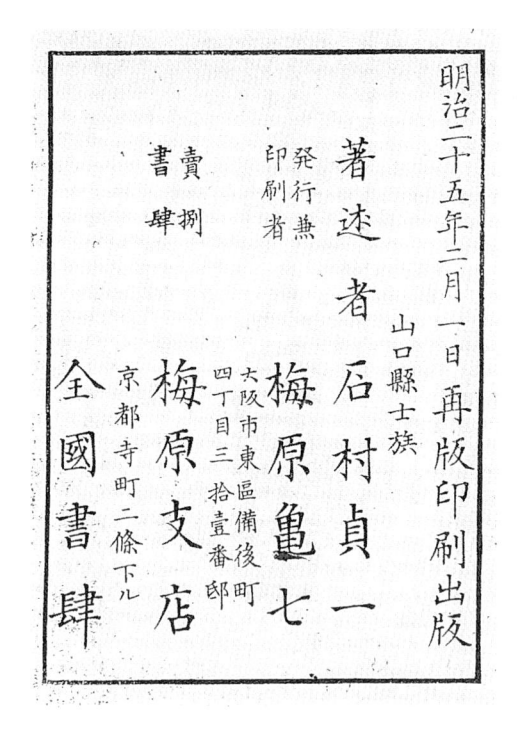

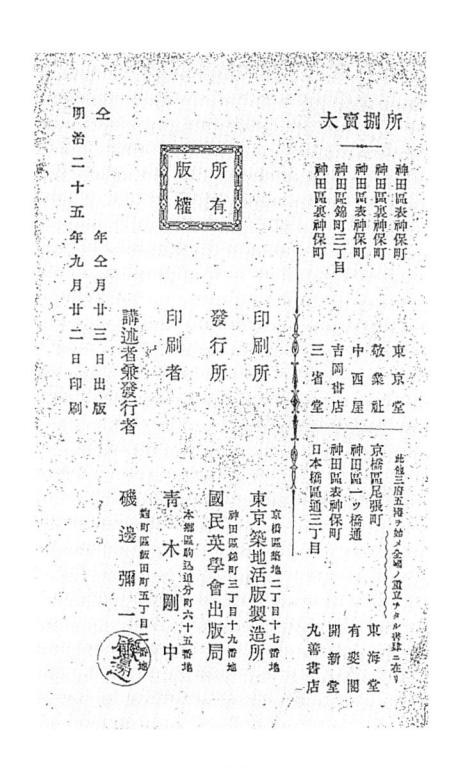

A－16（1893：明治26年）

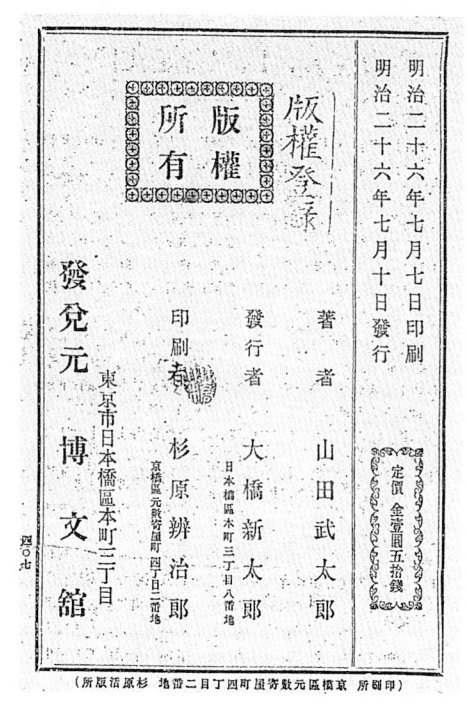

A－16（奥付）

A－17（1893：明治26年）

A－18（1893：明治26年）

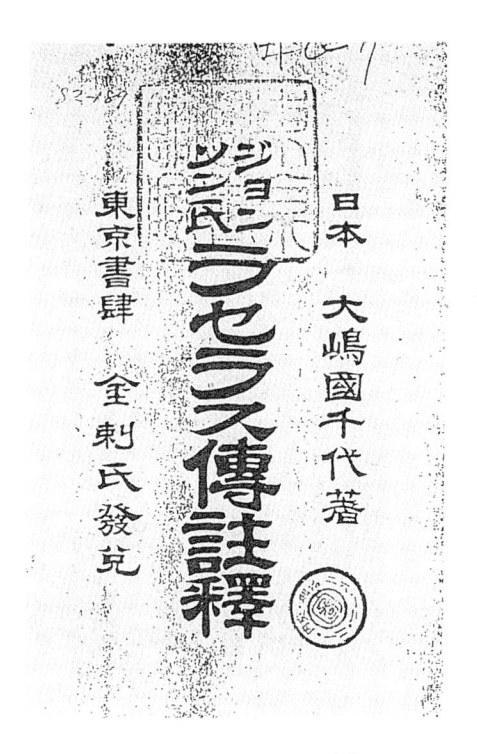

A−19 (1893:明治26年)

A−20 (1894:明治27年)　　　　　　　　　A−20 (奥付)

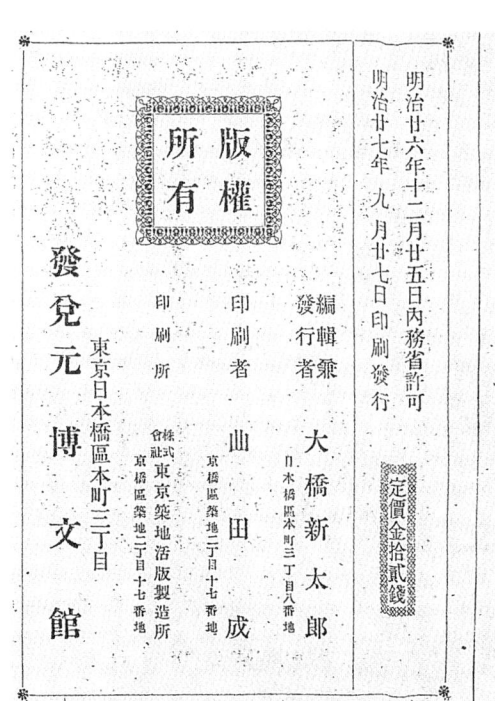

A−21（1894：明治27年）

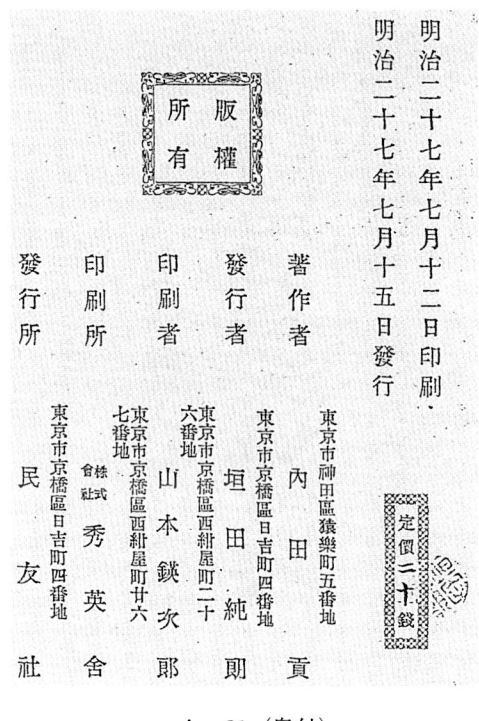

A−21（奥付）

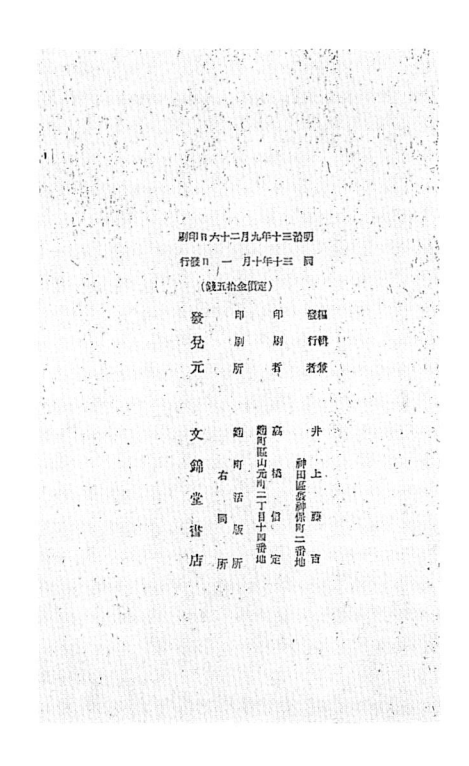

A−22（1897：明治30年）

A−22（奥付）

A−23（1900：明治33年）

A−24（1901：明治34年）

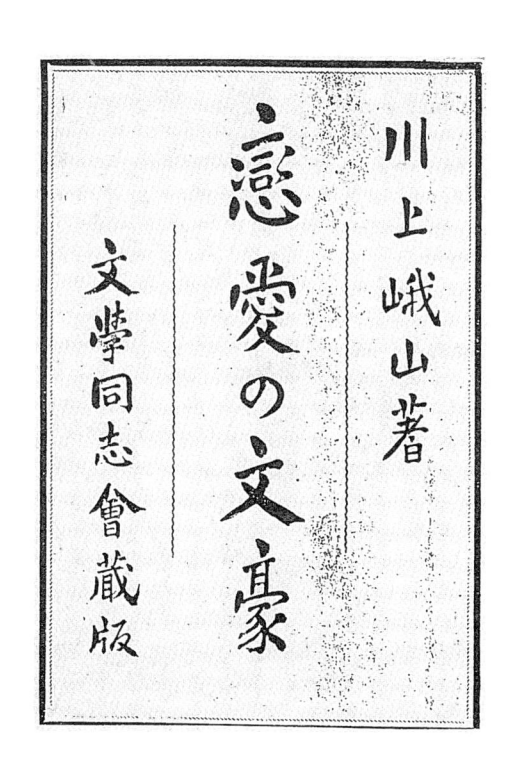

A−25（1902：明治35年）

THE
HISTORY OF RASSELAS
PRINCE OF ABYSSINIA
by
DR. SAMUEL JOHNSON

Translated and Annotated
by
SHIBANO ROKUSUKE
with
INTRODUCTION
by
UEDA BIN

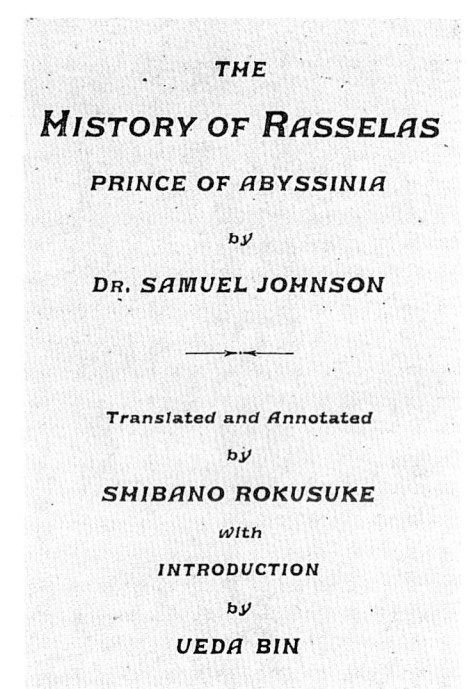

A-26 (1905：明治38年)

發兌

明治三十八年六月十七日印刷
明治三十八年六月二十日發行
明治三十八年十月十日再版發行

校閲者 文學士 上田 敏
譯述者發行 芝野 六助
印刷者 大日本圖書株式會社
代表取締役 宮□□□

東京市京橋區銀座壹丁目
大日本圖書株式會社

東京市京橋區銀座壹丁目
大阪市東區北久太郎町四丁目
大日本圖書株式會社支社

定價金四拾錢

A-26 （奥付）

The Lake English Classics

MACAULAY'S ESSAYS
ON
ADDISON AND JOHNSON

EDITED FOR SCHOOL USE
BY
ALPHONSO G. NEWCOMER
ASSOCIATE PROFESSOR OF ENGLISH IN THE LELAND STANFORD
JUNIOR UNIVERSITY

CHICAGO
SCOTT, FORESMAN AND COMPANY
1906

A-27 (1906：明治39年)

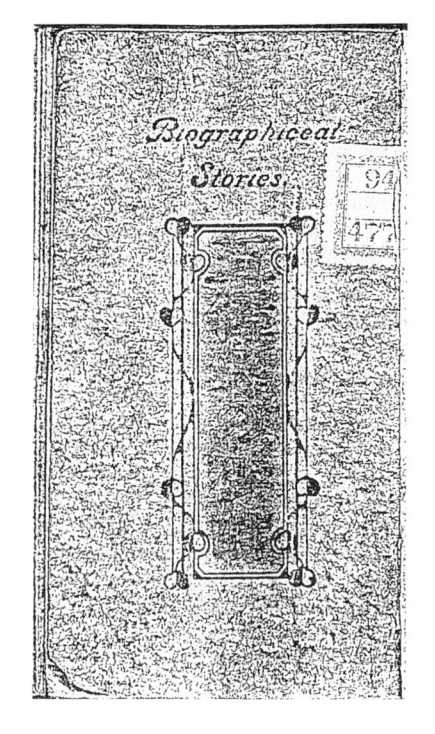

A-28（1907：明治40年）

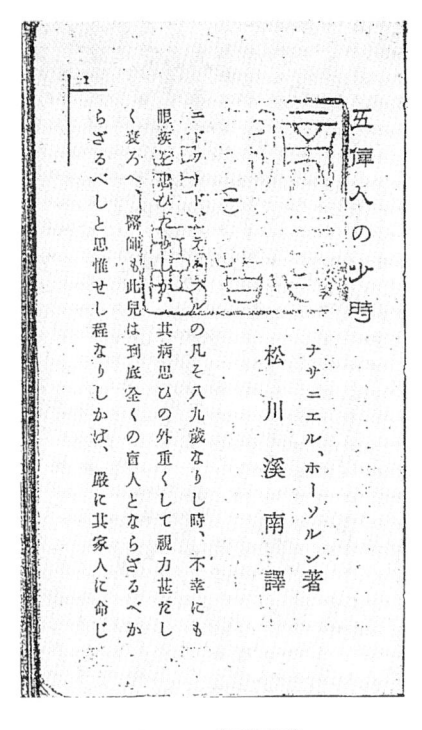

A-28（冒頭頁）

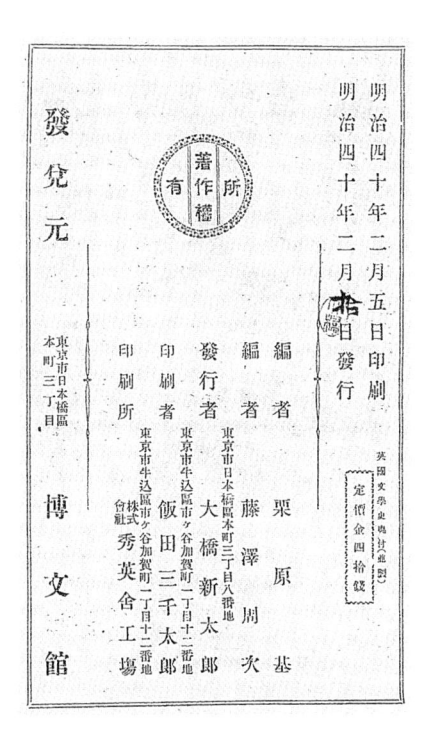

A-29（1907：明治40年）

A-29（奥付）

A－30（1907：明治40年）　　　　　　　　A－30（奥付）

A－31（1907：明治40年）　　　　　　　　A－31（奥付）

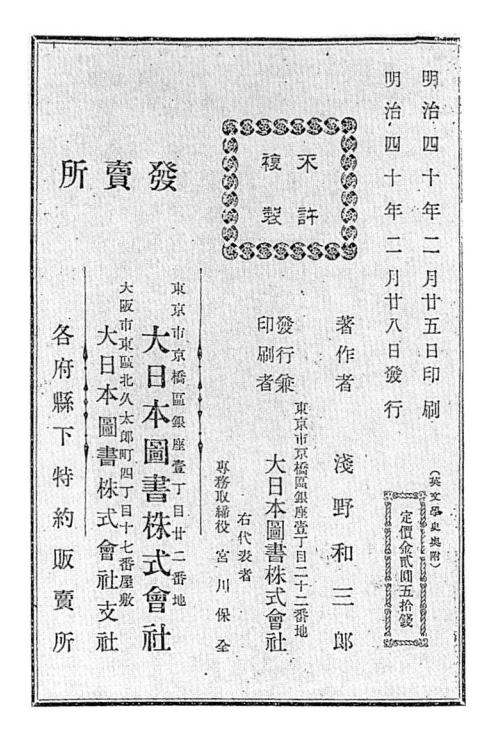

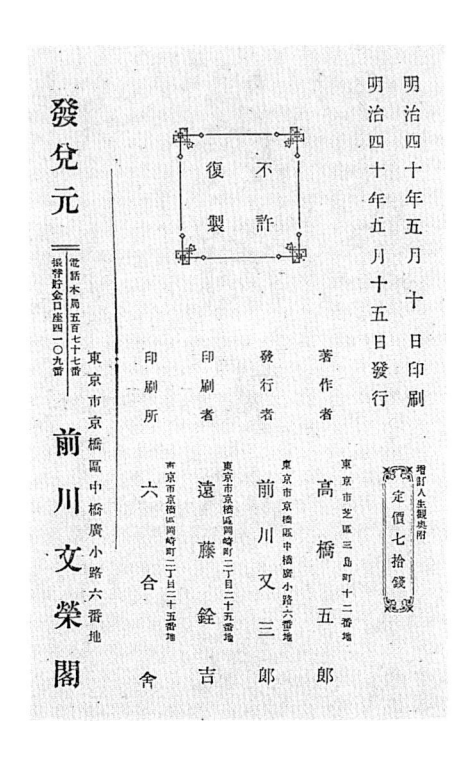

人生と健闘

田村逆水著

A-32 (1908：明治41年)

博士ジョンッシ原著

坂本大風譯編

ラセラス王子物語

東京 内外出版協會

A-33 (1909：明治42年)

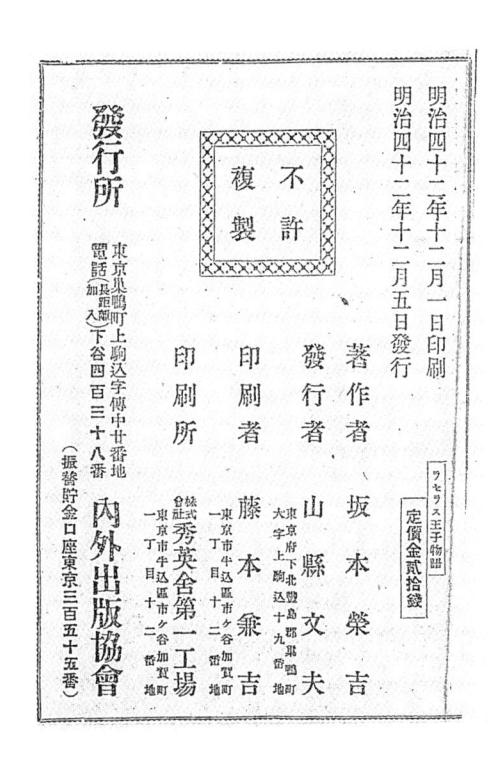

明治四十二年十二月一日印刷
明治四十二年十二月五日發行

〔ラセラス王子物語〕 定價金貳拾錢

不許複製

著作者　坂本榮吉
　　　　東京府北豐島郡巣鴨町大字上駒込十九番地

發行者　山縣文夫
　　　　東京市牛込區市ヶ谷加賀町一丁目十二番地

印刷者　藤本兼吉
　　　　東京市牛込區市ヶ谷加賀町一丁目十二番地

印刷所　株式會社秀英舍第一工場
　　　　東京市牛込區市ヶ谷加賀町一丁目十二番地

發行所　內外出版協會
　　　　東京市北豐島郡上駒込字傳中廿甘番地
　　　　電話（長距離）下谷四百三十八番
　　　　（振替貯金口座東京三百五十五番）

A-33 (奥付)

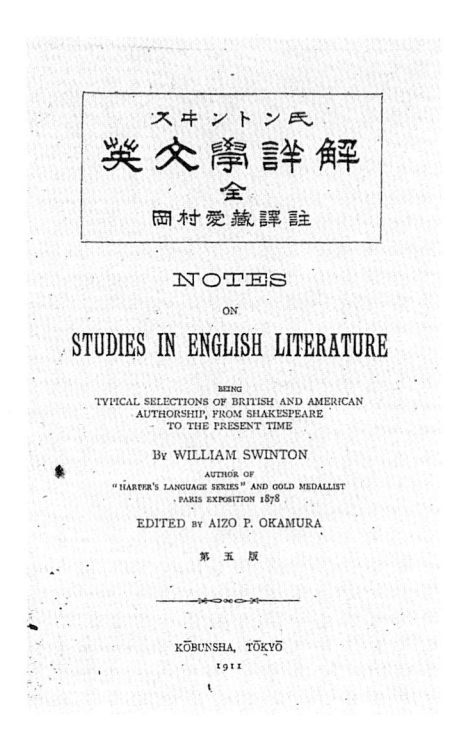

A－34（1911：明治44年）　　　　A－34（奥付）

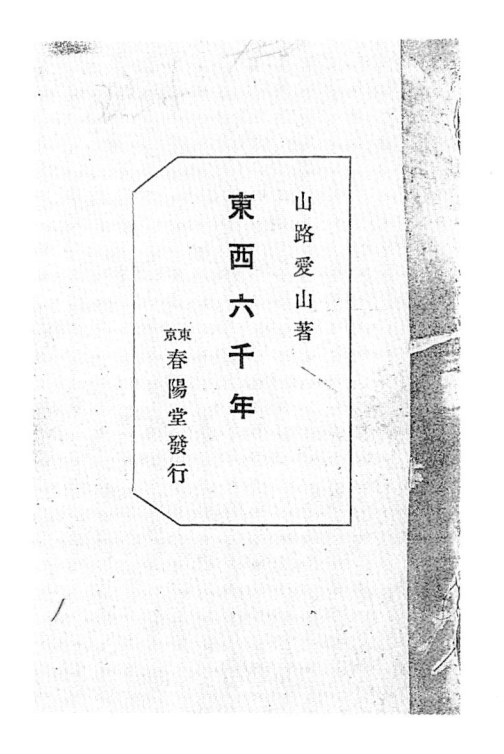

B－1（1916：大正5年）　　　　B－1（奥付）

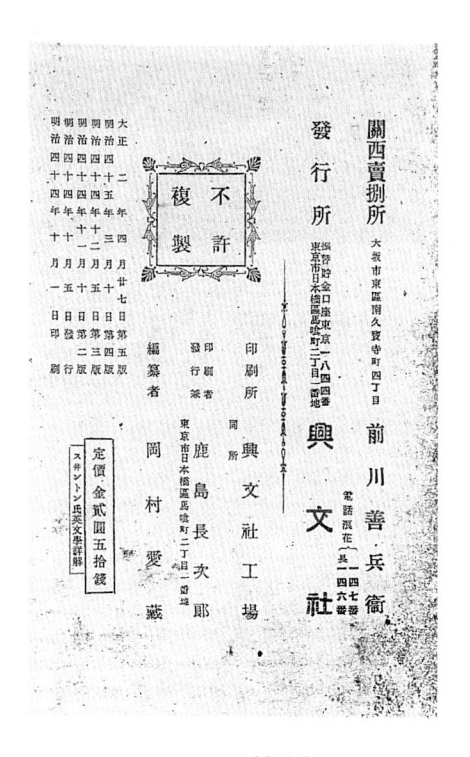

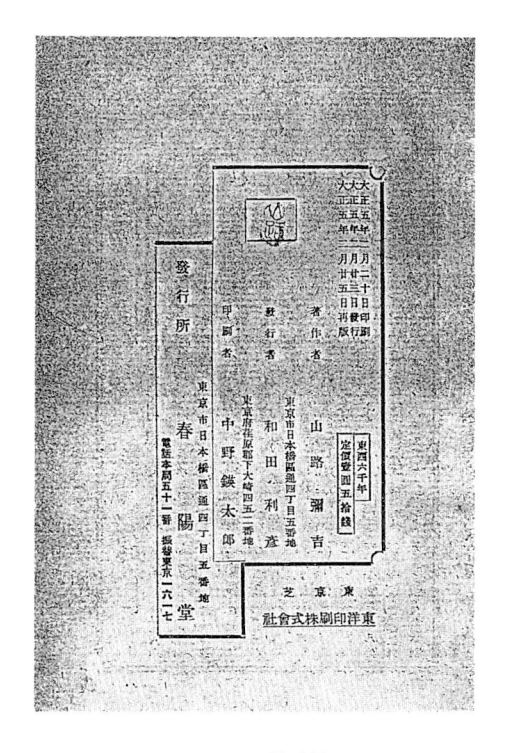

MACAULAY'S

LIFE OF SAMUEL JOHNSON

EDITED WITH NOTES AND AN INTRODUCTION
BY
WILLIAM SCHUYLER, A.M.
PRINCIPAL OF THE MCKINLEY HIGH SCHOOL, ST. LOUIS, MO.

New York
THE MACMILLAN COMPANY
LONDON: MACMILLAN & CO., LTD.
1922
All rights reserved

B-2 (1922：大正11年)

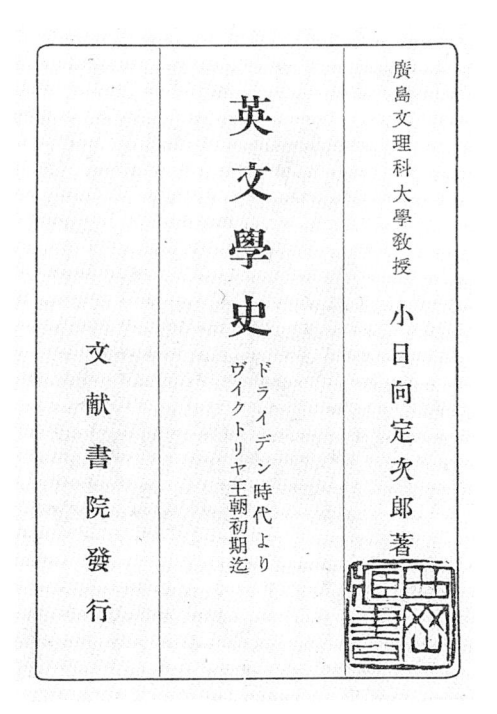

英文學史 ドライデン時代より ヴィクトリヤ王朝初期迄

廣島文理科大學教授 小日向定次郎 著

文獻書院發行

B-3 (1924：大正13年)

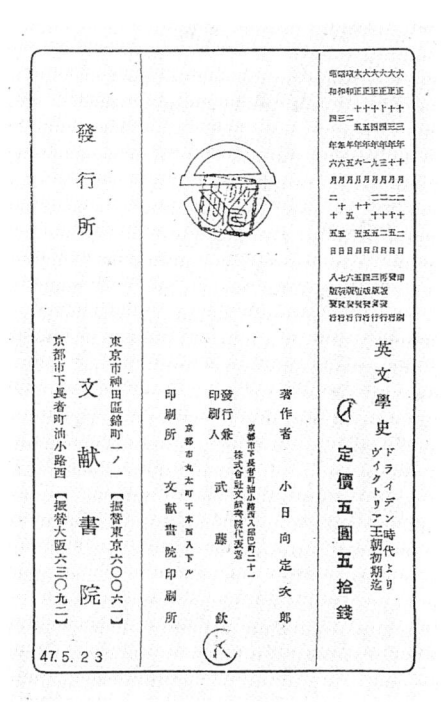

英文學史 ドライデン時代より ヴィクトリヤ王朝初期迄 定價五圓五拾錢

著作者　小日向定次郎
發行人　武藤　欽
印刷人
印刷所　文獻書院印刷所
發行所　文獻書院

B-3 (奥付)

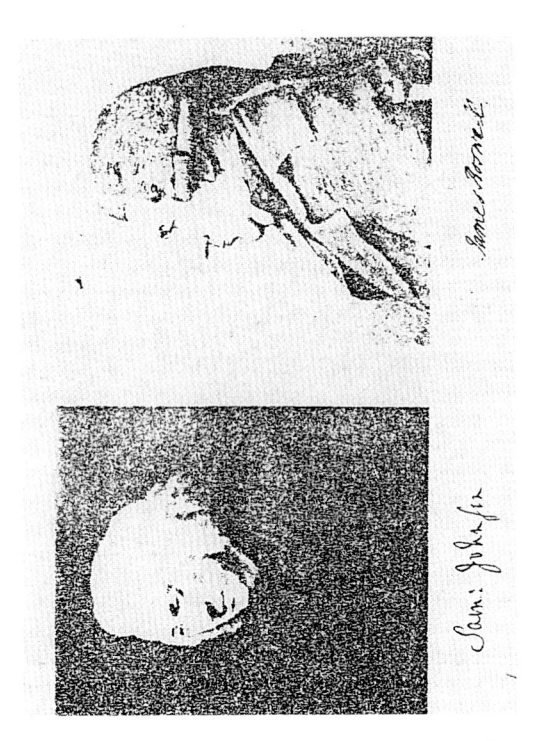

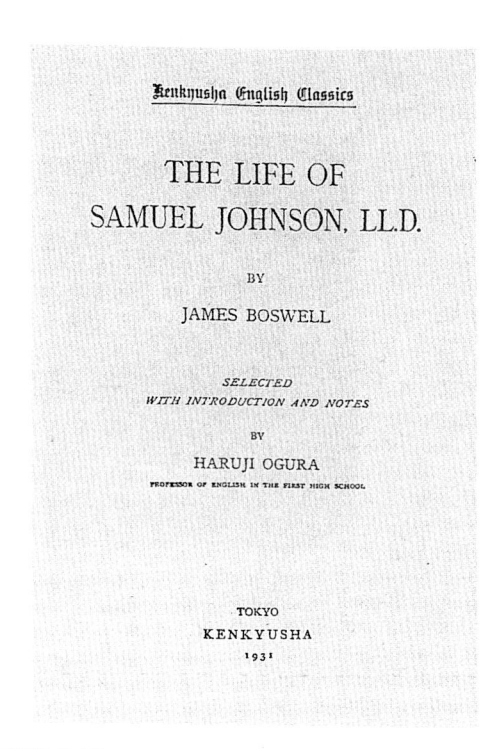

C-1 (1931：昭和6年)

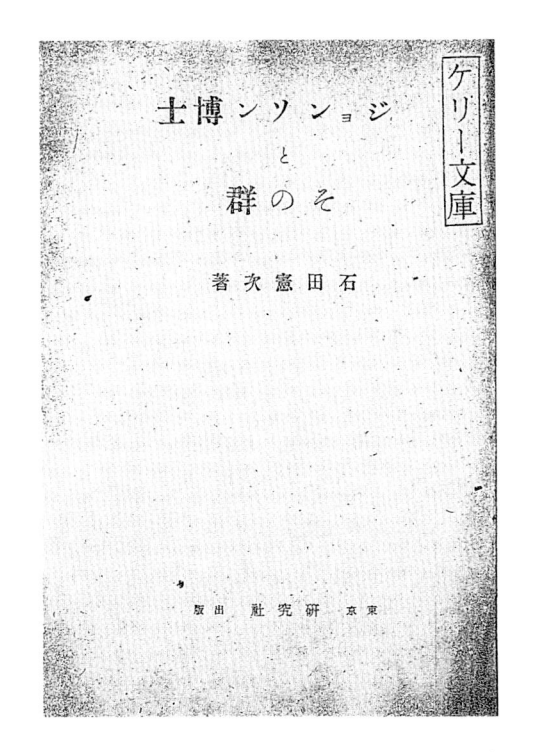

C-2 (1933：昭和8年)

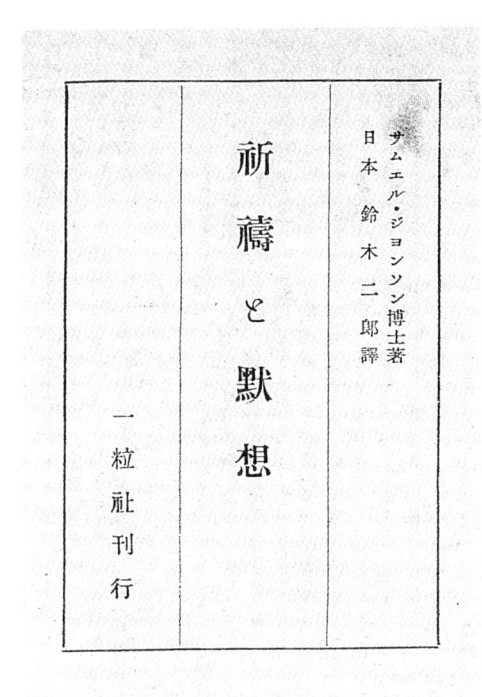

『ラセラス』受容史の研究(3)

C-3 (1933：昭和8年)

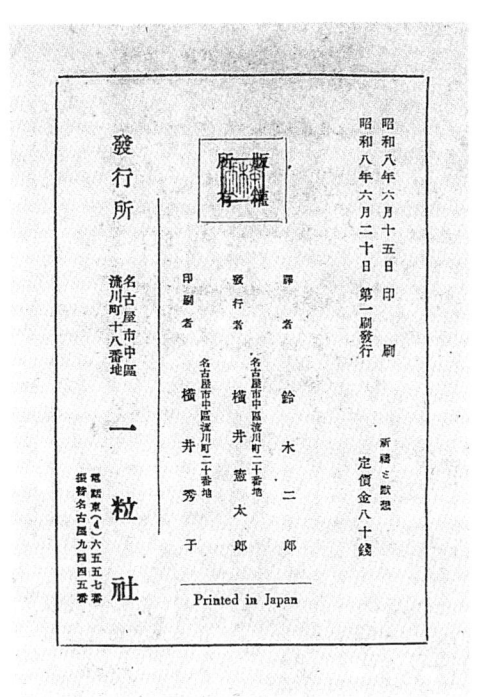

C-3 (奥付)

C-4 (1934：昭和9年)

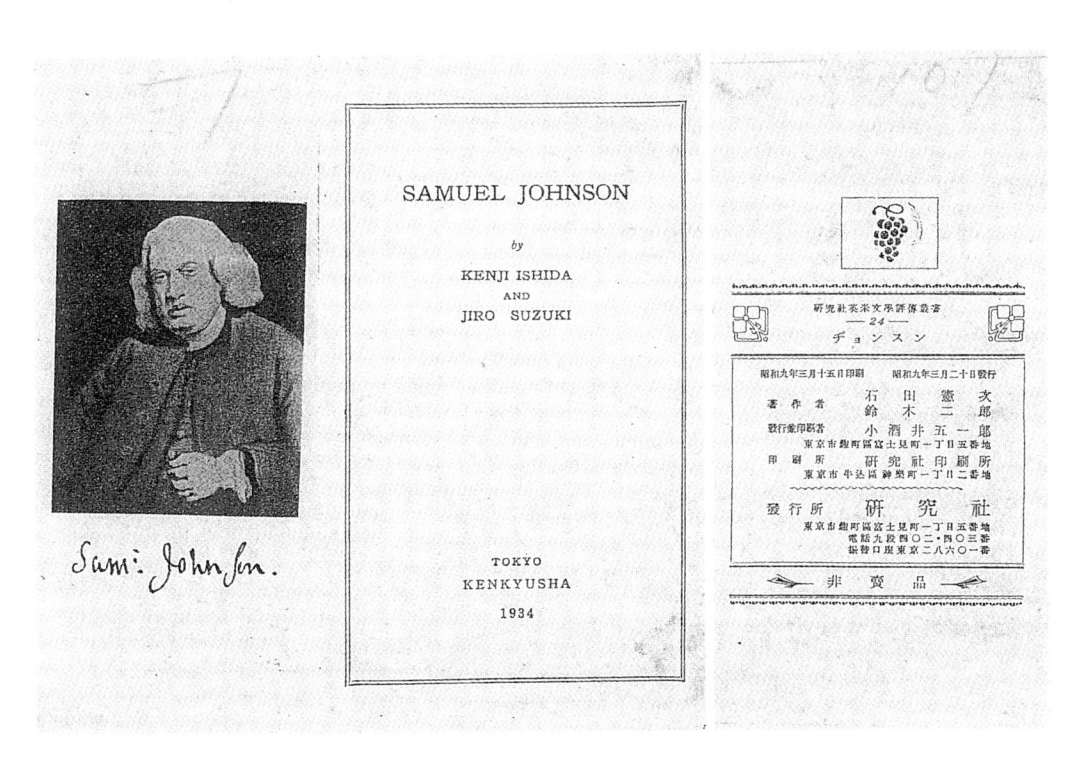

C-4 (奥付)

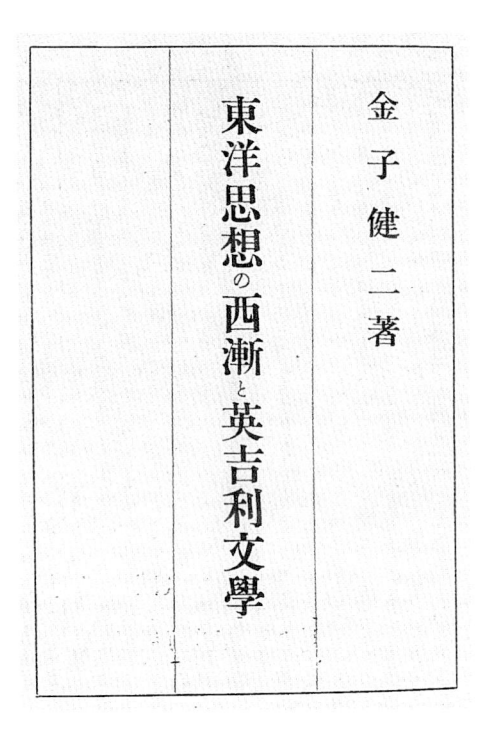

C-5 (1934：昭和9年)

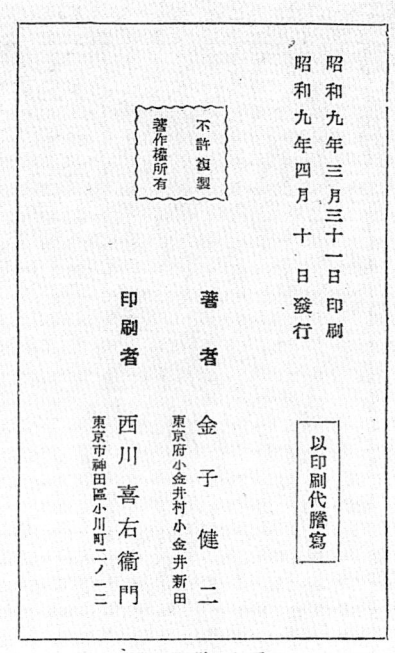

金子健二 著

東洋思想の西漸と英吉利文學

C-5 (奧付)

昭和九年三月三十一日印刷
昭和九年四月十日發行

不許複製
著作權所有

著者　金子健二
　　　東京府小金井村小金井新田

印刷者　西川喜右衞門
　　　東京市神田區小川町二ノ二

以印刷代謄寫

秀工社印刷行

C-6 (1935：昭和10年)

Boswell's
Life of Johnson

Selected and Annotated
by
Shun Katayama
Professor of English in the Osaka University of Commerce

HIRANO SHOTEN
Kyoto

C-6 (奧付)

昭和十年二月五日印刷
昭和十年二月十日發行

定價金壹圓

著者　片山　俊
發行者　平野慎之助
印刷者　京都市烏丸通今出川
印刷所　平野書店出版部
　　　　京都市烏丸通今出川

發行所　平野書店
　　　　京都市烏丸通今出川
　　　　振替大阪七四八七九番

C−7 (1941：昭和16年)

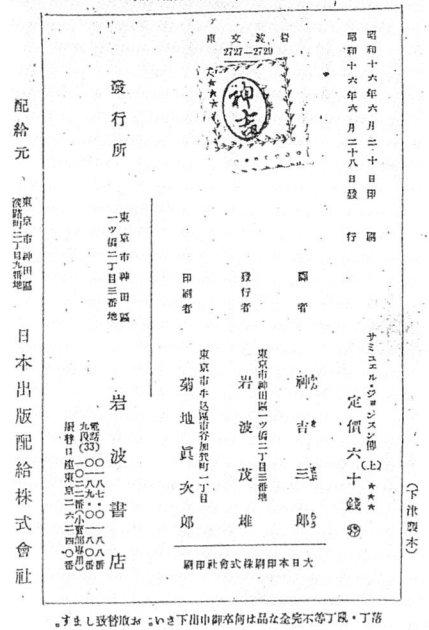

C−7 (奥付)

新英米文学評伝叢書

SAMUEL

JOHNSON

福原麟太郎

1972
東京 研究社 出版

C−8 (1972：昭和47年)

C−8 (奥付)

『ラセラス』受容史の研究(4)

The Reception-History of *Rasselas*; In the Case of the Editions (4)

　　This paper is the fourth instalment of the serial *The Reception-History of Rasselas: In the Case of the Editions*, which has been running in the preceding volumes of the present *Memoirs*. The editor was particularly fortunate in making the Kolb collection of the *Rasselas* editions a central part of the present paper. The research for this issue could not have been completed without the assistance and encouragement of professor Gwin J. Kolb of the University of Chicago, who kindly permitted its reproduction for the Japanese readership. In the first section (A), two books of *Rasselas* editions are introduced as a token of the editor's acknowledgement of this superb Johnson scholar. The next section (B) is devoted to the various kinds of the 37 editions which are based on the Kolb collection.Thirdly and finally, 3 Japanese printings are offered, not as an exhaustive survey, but as an additional contribution toward 'Johnson and his *Rasselas* in modern Japan' of the last issue. After the brief survey of these 42 items in all, the editor could not help being amazed at how long and widely human minds have been influenced and obssessed by this little oriental tale.

Keywords : Samuel Johnson, *Rasselas*, Kolb Collection, Editions, Chronological checklist, Meiji period.

　　本稿は，一連の「『ラセラス』受容史の研究」の第4弾として，さらなる『ラセラス』版本とその関連文献のご紹介である。本稿では，シカゴ大学のコルブ教授からご提供頂いた多数の資料のうちから，そのコレクションの一部を

先生のご了解をえてご紹介して見たい。まず最初には（A），先生より頂いた2冊の『ラセラス』本を掲げて同学相求める交友の記念とし，次いで（B）では先生の蔵書から合計37冊，最後に前号の日本におけるジョンソン文献の補足として3冊の和書を追記した。これら合計42冊を検討して見ると，ジョンソンの物した一冊の東洋物語が広く長く人心に与えてきた人気と影響に改めて驚かされる。

I．Gwin J. Kolb Collection of *Rasselas*

われわれは日頃よく〈一冊の本〉という言葉を目にする。それはただ座右の書（'a companionable book'）として愛読するだけでなく、当人その人にとっては大きた衝撃となってその人生をも変え、方向づける不可思議な魔力をも持っているようである。筆者にとっても例外ではない。今日わが国においては顧みる者も少ない『ラセラス』というささやかな1冊がさまざまな学恩の輪を広げ、交友の往来を密にして、なお尽きることがない。今は亡き碩学フリーマン先生（Dr. J.D. Fleeman, Oxford Univ.）との親交の発端もこの書であったし、今日なお師として仰ぐコルブ先生（Dr. Gwin J. Kolb, Chester D. Tripp Professor Emeritus in the Humanities, University of Chicago）とのご縁もこのささやかな本（'a little book'）なしには頂けなかったものである。先生は米国第一のジョンソン学者であるのみならず、『ラセラス』版本の収集家（the Hunter & Collector）でもある。ここに筆者にお送り下さった二冊の『ラセラス』本を最初に記念としてご紹介しておきたい。第5版（1775, 1,000部）は筆者もこれまで、未だ刮目の機に浴しなかったものである。

1．A－1（1775：安永4年）
　THE PRINCE OF ABISSINIA.／A TALE.／THE FIFTH EDITION.／LONDON:／PRINTED FOR W. STRAHAM, J. DODSLEY,／AND E. JOHNSTON.／MDCCLXXV.

2．A－2（1990：平成2年）
　SAMUEL JOHNSON／Rasselas and Other Tales／*EDITED BY GWIN J. KOLB*／NEW HAVEN AND LONDON: YALE UNIVERSITY PRESS／1990

II．1759（宝暦9）年～1994（平成6）年

本稿では、まずコルブ・コレクションから、版権所有者版（Propriater's Edition）の第2版、第5版、第7版、第8版を挙げておきたい。初版（1759）、3版（1760）、4版（1766）、6版（1783）、9版（1793）はすでにご紹介したので、これで1759年の*Rasselas*第1版から第10版（1798）までのプロプライアター版はご紹介したことになる。その後は新版（New Edition）となる。B－11（1791）、B－15（1800）、B－17（1803）、B－24（1811）はアメリカ版である。B－7（1787）、B－14（1798）、B－16（1802）は仏語版であるが、B－14（1798）は本稿(1)で紹介したB－10（1796）と、またB－16（1802）は本稿(1)のB－11（1799）とは挿絵が同一であり、それぞれ前者の仏語版であることが分かる。B－19（1804）とB－28（1818）は英文ではあるが出版元は東洋物語の発祥地パリである。また、B－27（1817）は本稿(1)C－25（1828）のRichard Westallの同一版画である。B－29（1818）はスペイン語、B－32（1823）、B－33（1825）はイタリア語版である。N.D.版として挙げておいたB－35はCooke版であって、1799年、あるいはそれ以後のものと思われる。B－36（1993）とB－37（1994）は入手可能な近年の出版物なので敢えて追記した。

さらに，『ラセラス』批評史の立場から調査されたE. トマーケン教授（Professor Edward Tomarken）によれば，合計38冊の次の『ラセラス』版本の序文（Introduction）等にその論考が見られる。(See "A History of *Rasselas* Criticism 1759-1986," & "A Chronological Checklist of Rasselas Criticism 1759-1986." in *Johnson, Rasselas, and the Choice of Criticism*, The Univ. Press of Kentucky, 1989.)

　1787, Dublin; 1803, Dublin; 1805, London; 1807, London, ed. Leigh Hunt; 1809, London; 1812, Edinburgh; 1815, London; 1823, London, ed. Sir Walter Scott; 1824, Edinburgh; 1838, London, ed. Charles Till; 1843, London; 1850, Philadelphia, Hogan and Thompson; 1860, London, Longmans; 1869, London, ed. Rev. William West; 1873, Philadelphia, Yale University; 1879, Oxford, ed. Alfred Milnes; 1879, London, Whittaker & Co.; 1884, London, George Routledge & Son, ed. Henry Morley; 1884, London, Elliot Stock, ed. Dr. James Macaulay; 1887, London, Oxford up, ed. George B. Hill; 1888, London, Cassell & Co., ed. Henry Morley; 1891, Boston and New York, Leach, Shewell and Sanborn, ed. Fred N. Scott; 1894, London, Murray, ed. Walter A. Raleigh; 1895, New York, Henry Holt, ed. Oliver F. Emerson; 1900, London, ed. Justin Hannaford; 1905, London, John Lang, ed. Hannaford Bennett; 1906, London, ed. C.S. Fearenside; 1910, London, W.B. Cline, ed. A.J.F. Collins; 1926, London, J.M. Dent & Sons, ed. G.K. Chesterton; 1927, Oxford, Clarendon Press, ed. R.W.Chapman; 1930, New York, E.P.Dutton & Co., ed. philip Henderson; 1962, Great Neck, N.Y.,Barron's Educational Series, ed. Warren L. Kleisehauer; 1962, New York, Appleton-Century-Crofts, ed. Qwin J. Kolb; 1968, New York, Oxford UP, ed. John Hardy; 1971, New York, Oxford UP, ed. Geoffrey Tillotson; 1975, Edinburgh, Folio Society, ed. Gilbert Phelps; 1976, Baltimore, Penguin Co., ed. D.J. Enright; 1977, Delhi, Doaba House, ed. R.W. Desai;

3．B－1（1759：宝暦9年, 2nd Edn.）

　THE PRINCE OF ABISSINIA.／A TALE.／IN TWO VOLUMES.／VOL.1.／THE SECOND EDITION.／LONDON:／Printed for R. and J. DODSLEY, in Pall-Mall;／and W.JOHNSTON, in Ludgate-Street.／MDCCLIX.

4．B－2（1775：安永4年, 5th Edn.）

　THE PRINCE OF ABISSINIA.／A TALE.／THE FIFTH EDITION.／LONDON:／PRINTED FOR W. STRAHAN, J. DODSLEY,／AND E. JOHNSTON.／MDCCLXXV.

5．B－3（1785：天明5年）

　THE PRINCE OF ABISSINIA.／A TALE.／BY SAMUEL JOHNSON, L.L.D.／MENTZ and FRANKFORT, Printed for J.F. SCHILLER; and Sold／by VARRENTRAPP Junior and WENNER.／MDCCLXXXV.

6．B－4（1786：天明6年, 7th Edn.）

　THE PRINCE OF ABISSINIA. ／A TALE. ／THE SEVENTH EDITION. ／LONDON: ／PRINTED FOR J.F. AND C.RIVINGTON, J. DODSLEY, T. LONGMAN, AND／G. AND T. WILKIE.／MDCCLXXXVI.

7．B－5（1787：天明7年）

　RASSELAS,／PRINCE／OF／ABISSINIA:／A TALE.／BY S. JOHNSON, L.L.D.／LONDON:

／PRINTED FOR JOSEPH WENMAN, NO.144／FLEET-STREET.／M,DCC,LXXVII.

8．B－6（1787：天明7年）

THE PRINCE OF ABISSINIA.／A TALE.／BY SAMUEL JOHNSON, L.L.D.／IN TWO VOLUMES.／VOL.1.／DUBLIN:／PRINTED FOR SHEPPARD AND NUGENT,／ANND-STREET, STEPHEN'S-GREEN.／M,DCC,LXXXVII.

9．B－7（1787：天明7年）

LA／VRAIE MANIERE／D'APPRENDRE／UNE LANGUE QUELCONQUE,／VIVANTE OU MORTE,／*PAR le moyen de la Langue Francoise*;／SUITE DE LA GRAMMAIRE ANGLOISE,／OU／Traduction littérale d'un ouvrage Anglois, intitulé／THE PRINCE OF ABISSINIA,／HISTOIRE DE RASSELAS, PRINCE D'ABYSSINIE;／TOME PREMIER.／*A PARIS*;／M.DCC.LXXXVII.

10．B－8（1789：寛政1年）

THE HISTORY OF RASSELAS,／PRINCE OF *ABBISSINIA*.／BY SAMUEL JOHNSON, L.L.D.／A NEW EDITION.／EDINBURGH:／PRINTED FOR WILLIAM CREECH.／M.DCC.LXXXIX.

11．B－9（1790：寛政2年, 8th Edn.）

THE PRINCE OF ABISSINIA.／A TALE.／THE EIGHTH EDITION.／LONDON:／PRINTED FOR J. F. AND C. RIVINGTON,／J.DODSLEY, T.LONGMAN, AND／G. AND T. WILKIE,／MDCCXC.

12．B－10（1790：寛政2年）

RASSELAS;／PRINCE OF ABISSINIA.／A TALE.／*BY DR. JOHNSON.*／IN TWO VOLUMES.／VOL.1／A NEW EDITION.／LONDON:／PRINTED FOR T. JOHNSTONE,／W. TAYLOR, AND J. DAVIES.／MDCC XC.

13．B－11（1791：寛政3年, USA Edn.）

THE PRINCE OF ABISSINIA.／A TALE.／BY SAMUEL JOHNSON, LL.D.／THE TWO VOLUMES COMPLETE IN ONE.／VOLUME THE FIRST.／*PHILADELPHIA*:／PRINTED BY FRANCIS BAILEY.No.116／MARKET STREET, AND T.LANG,／No 21, CHURCH-ALLEY.／M DCC XCI.

14．B－12（1792：寛政4年）

RASSELAS,／PRINCE OF ABISSINIA.／A TALE.／*BY S. JOHNSON, L.L.D.*／A NEW EDITION.／LONDON:／PRINTED FOR H. D. SYMONDS, No 20, PATER／NOSTER-ROW.

15．B－13（1795：寛政7年）

THE HISTORY OF RASSELAS,／PRINCE OF ABISSINIA.／*A TALE.*／BY DR. JOHNSON,／TWO VOLUMES IN ONE.／EMBELLISHED WITH A PORTRAIT OF THE AUTHOR.／LONDON:／PRINTED UNDER THE INSPECTION OF THE LITERARY ASSOCIATION,／AND SOLD BY JOHN CRESWICK, AND CO.／AGENTS TO THE SOCIETY／1795.

16．B－14（1798：寛政10年）

RASSELAS,／*PRINCE D'ABISSINIE.*／ROMAN.／TRADUIT DE L'ANGLOIS DE DR. JOHNSON, PAR LE／COMTE DE FOUCHECOUR.／ENRICHE DE TAILLE DOUCES.／*A LONDRES*:／CHEZ M.M.／LACKINGTON, ALLEN, ET COMP.／TEMPLE OF THE MUSES,

FINSBURY SQUARE.／1798.

17.　B－15（1800：寛政12年）

　　THE HISTORY OF RASSELAS,／PRINCE OF ABISSINIA:／*A TALE.*／BY SAMUEL JOHNSON, L.L.D.／TO WHICH IS PREFIXED,／*LIFE OF THE AUTHOR*:／BY F.W.BLAGDON, Esq.／*Second American Edition.*／BRIDGEPORT:／PRINTED AND SOLD, BY S.BACKUS, & Co.

18.　B－16（1802：享和2年）

　　RASSELAS,／*PRINCE D'ABISSINIE.*／ROMAN.／Traduit de l'Anglois／DU／DR. JOHNSON,／PAR LE／*Compte De Fouchecour.*／LONDON:／Printed for／LACKINGTON, ALLEN, AND CO.／Temple of the Muses,／Finsbury Square.／1802.

19.　B－17（1803：享和3年）

　　RASSELAS,／PRINCE OF ABISSINIA:／A TALE.／*BY S. JOHNSON, L.L.D.／First American Edition.／HARTFORD*：Printed For and Sold by Oliver D. Cooke.／1803,／*Lincoln & Gleason, Printers.*

20.　B－18（1804：享和4年）

　　RASSELAS,／PRINCE OF ABISSINIA:／BY DR. JOHNSON,／PRINTED WITH PATENT TYPES.／IN A MANNER／NEVER BEFORE ATTEMPTED.／Rusher's Edition.／BANBURY:／PRINTED FOR P.RUSHER;／AND SOLD BY MR.BUDD, AT THE CROWN AND／MITRE, PALL-MALL; MR.MILLER,49 BEMARLE-STREET; MR.TEGG,III／CHEAPSIDE, LONDON; AND／BY MR. J.RUSHER,／READING.／1804／GHENEY, PRINTER, HIGH-STREET, BANBURY.

21.　B－19（1804：享和4年）

　　THE HISTORY OF RASSELAS.／PRINCE of ABISSINIA:／A TALE.／BY DR. JOHNSON.／A New Edition in one volume.／PARIS:／Printed for THEOPHILUS BARROIS junior,／Bookseller, Quay Voltaire, no.3.／1804.

22.　B－20（1806：文化3年）

　　THE HISTORY OF RASSELAS,／PRINCE OF ABISSINIA:／*A TALE.*／BY SAMUEL JOHNSON, L.L.D.／EDINBURGH:／PRINTED FOR BELL & BRADFUTE, JAMES M`CLIESH, AND／WILLIAM BLACKWOOD;／GILBERT & HODGES, DUBLIN; AND S.CAMPBELL,／NEW YORK.／1806.

23.　B－21（1809：文化6年）

　　RASSELAS by DR. JOHNSON.／*LONDON.／Published by W.Suttaby／B. Crosby & C. Scotcherd & Letterman, Stationers Court.／and C'Lorrall Charing Cross.*／1809.

24.　B－22（1809：文化6年）

　　RASSELAS; *A TALE.*／BY SAMUEL JOHNSON, L.L.D.／WITH／THE LIFE OF／THE AUTHOR.／EDINBURGH:／*Printed by George Ramsay and Company,*／FOR J.THOMSON, JUN. AND COMPANY, EDINBURDH;／AND JOHN MURRAY, LONDON.／1809.

25.　B－23（1810：文化7年）

　　THE BRITISH NOVELISTS;／WITH／*AN ESSAY;*／AND／PREFACES,／BIOGRAPHICAL AND CRITICAL.／BY／*MRS. BARBAULD.*／VOL.XXVI.／*LONDON*: 1810.

26. B−24 (1811：文化8年)

　　THE HISTORY OF RASSELAS,／PRINCE OF ABISSINIA:／BY SAMUEL JOHNSON, L.L.D.／WITH／LIFE OF THE AUTHOR,／BY F,W,BLAGDON, ESQ.／To which are added,／JOHNSON'S MISCELLANEOUS POEMS.／*BOSTON.*／PRINTED BY J.BELCHER／1811.

27. B−25 (1814：文化11年)

　　RASSELAS, ／ PRINCE OF ABISSINIA; ／ A TALE. ／ BY DR. JOHNSON. ／ LEEDS: ／ PRINTED BY B.DEWHIRST, AND SOLD BY／M. MARSDEN, AND CO.／1814.

28. B−26 (1816：文化13年)

　　RASSELAS,／PRINCE OF ABISSINIA.／by／Dr JOHNSON／1816.

29. B−27 (1817：享保2年)

　　RASSELAS ／ BY ／ SAMUEL JOHNSON, L.L.D. ／ EMBELISHED WITH ENGRAVINGS ／ FROM THE DESIGNS OF／RICHARD WESTALL R.A.／LONDON:／PUBLISHED BY JOHN SHARP. PICCADILLY.／1817.

30. B−28 (1818：文政1年)

　　RASSELAS,／PRINCE OF ABYSSINIA／A TALE／BY DR JOHNSON.／WITH THE LIFE OF AUTHOR／PARIS／SOLD BY F. LOUIS, BOOKSELLER,／AT HIS FRENCH AND ENGLISH LIBRARY／rue Hautefeuille, No.10.／1818.

31. B−29 (1818：文政1年)

　　RASSELAS／PRINCIPE DE ABISINIA.／ROMANCE.／TRADUCIDO DEL INGLES／DEL／DOCTOR JOHNSON.／POR EL／*EV. DON FELIPE FERNANDEZ, A.M.*／Y／andador de la Real Sociedad Economica de Xerez／de la Frontera.／IMPRESO EN LONDRES,／Por Henrique Bryer, Bridge Street, Blackfriar,／A EXPENSAS DE FRANCISCO WINGRAVE, Y DE／DICHO REV. TRADUCTOR.／1818.

32. B−30 (1820：文政3年)

　　THE HISTORY OF RASSELAS,／PRINCE OF ABISSINIA.／BY SAMUEL JOHNSON, LL.D.／ ALMORAN AND HAMET. ／ AN ORIENTAL TALE. ／ BY DR. HAWKESWORTH. ／ J. M'CREERY, Printer,／Black-Horse-Court, London.

33. B−31 (1822：文政5年)

　　RASSELAS,／PRINCE OF ABISSINIA;／A TALE;／*BY DR. JOHNSON.*／STEREOTYPE EDITION.／LONDON:／*Stereotyped by Andrew Wilson, Camden Town*／PRINTED AND SOLD BY DEAN & MUNDAY, 35, THREADNEEDLE STREET／1822.

34. B−32 (1823：文政6年)

　　RASSELAS, ／ PRINCIPE D'ABISSINIA: ／ TRADOTTO DALL' INGLESE ／ DEL SIGNOR DOTTOR JOHNSON.／LONDRA:／PRESSO G.e W.B. WHITTAKER,／1823.

35. B−33 (1825：文政8年)

　　STORIA DI RASSELAS／PRINCIPE D'ABISSINIA／DI／S. JOHNSON／*Tradotta dall' Inglese*／DA／LIVORNO／／DALLA STAMPERIA DI G.P. POZZOLINI／1825.

36. B−34 (1846：弘化3年)

　　THE HISTORY OF RASSELAS, PRINCE OF ABYSSINIA.／A TALE.／BY／SAMUEL JOHNSON, LL.D. ／ LONDON: ／ SOLD AT THE DEPOSITORY OF THE SOCIETY, ／ GREAT

QUEEN STREET, LINCOLN'S INNFIELDS; AT 4, ROYAL EXCHANGE／AND BY ALL BOOKSELLERS.／1846.

37. B－35 (N.D. COOKE'S Edn.)

THE HISTORY OF RASSELAS,／PRINCE OF ABISSINIA.／*A TALE.*／BY DR. JOHNSON.／TWO VOLUMES IN ONE.／Cooke's Edition.／EMBELLISHED WITH SUPERB EMGRAVINGS.／LONDON.／Printed for C.COOKE, Paternoster Row,／by J.Adlard, Duke Street,／Smithfield, and sold／by all the Booksellers in Great Britain／and Ireland.

38. B－36 （1993：平成5年）

Ellis Cornelia Knight／DINARBAS／Edited by Ann Messenger／EAST LANSING／COLLEAGUES PRESS／1993

39. B－37 （1994：平成6年）

Samuel Johnson／THE HISTORY OF RASSELAS,／PRINCE OF ABISSINIA／Ellis Cornelia Knight／DINARBAS; A TALE／*Edited by*／LYNNE MELOCCARO／University of Rochester, New York／EVERYMAN／J.M.DENT・LONDON／CHARLES E. TUTTLE／VERMONT

Ⅲ．明治期（1868，明元～1911，明44）

前号，(3)においてご紹介した明治期の版本に加えて，次の3書を挙げておきたい。C－1高橋本では，立身伝中の一人として「文章家 ジョンソン」がある。他には詩人として「ゴルズミス」(Oliver Goldsmith, 1728－74) が紹介されている。閲読の機会は逸したが，本書は多分，前号(3)のA－4，中村訳『西国童子鑑』やA－6，尾崎訳纂の『泰西名家幼伝』と同類のものと思われる。中村訳本はその表題に「ハルペル氏刊行」，また尾崎本では，凡例に「本書ハ専ラ米国ニウヨーク府ハーパー及ビブラサー社出版ノ〈ジ，ボイフッド，ヲフ，グレート，マン〉ト題セル書ニ拠リ傍ラ諸書ヲ参見シテ訳纂セル者トス」とあるとおり，これら2書の原本はJohn G. Edgar, *The Boyhood of Great Men*（New York: Harper & Brothers, 1855) である。この書もハーバード大学図書館（Harvard College Library, Harvard University）にただ1冊痛しい姿で所蔵されているのみである。("This book is 'too fragile to photocopy.'") C－2増田編本には（三）「ボズウェルに与へて其不和なりし父との仲直りを賀する書」(p.5) と（十）「人生の航海」(p.65) がある。この（十）の原文はThe *Rambler* 102（Saturday, 9 March 1751）であって『日本英学新誌』（明治25年3月～同26年1月第6巻第69号p.50～56に「S.K.生訳，編者（増田）閲」として訳されているものの再録である。C－3高橋訳には「交友の快楽」(p.100) および「交友の秘訣」(p.108) と題してサミュエル・ジョンソン博士の友情観が紹介されている。また，藤井哲氏のご指摘によれば，明治35 (1902) 年，警醒社発行の松村介石著『人物短評』に「サムエル・ジョンソン」の記事が，明治37 (1904) 年2月の弘文社発行の正岡猶一著『天才の失恋』に「ジョンソン」の一章 (pp.41-62) がある由である。(Tetsu Fujii, "A List of Johnson and Boswell Studies in Japan: Those Published in Book Form from 1871 to 1997," *The Bulletin of Central Research Institute*, Fukuoka University, No.208 〔Humanities and Social Science〕, March 1998, pp. 1-84.) なお，戦前の昭和期，とりわけ8，9年頃のジョンソンとその『ラセラス』への関心の背後には皇紀2600年の当時の日本と3000年の歴史を誇る非白人国エチオピアとの関係があった。エチオピア（アビシニア）の王子アベベと黒田子爵令嬢との結婚話しが話題となったこともあった。（日本ナイル・エチオピア学会「JANESニュースレター」，(No. 6〔1996.12〕，26参照）

また，同誌に紹介されている山田一広著『知っておきたいエチオピアの実像』（ほるぷ出版，1992）では1884（明治14）年に田村左衛士が『アビシニアの王子ヨハネス伝』を訳したとあるがどうであろうか。これは1890（明治23）年の田村訳『アビシニアの王子ラセラス伝』のことであろう。本多顕彰著の評伝『S・ジョンソン』（研究社叢書，昭和9年）が刊行されたものもこの時期であった。

　さらに，付記しておくべきことは，広く使用され，多大の影響を及ぼしたと考えられる明治期とその後の英語教科書のうちにジョンソン関連の記事を探してみると，頻度は少ないものの，興味深い記事が見られる。SANDERS' UNION FOURTH READER: BY CHARLES W. SANDERS, M.A., (New York and Chicago: Ivison, Blakeman & Co., 1863) には，*The Vanity of Wealth* と題して *The Vanity of Human Wishes* (1749) からの抜粋がある（Pp.380-81）。また，*Idler* から引用した格言（p.378）やジョンソン自身への言及（p.392）が見られる。岡倉由三郎著『ぐろうぶりいだ』(THE GLOBE READERS, Arranged in Grades By Okakura Yoshisaburo, Book Five, Tokyo: Dainihon-Tosho-Kabushiki-Kaisha, 1908, 1st edn, 1907) の第21課，第22課に *Dr. Johnson* と題して，有名な Uttoxeter market のエピソードが紹介されている（Pp.81-89）。また，神田乃武著『クラウン，リーダー，第五』(KANDA'S CROWN READERS, BOOK FIVE (Sanseido, 1916) の第24課には「ジョンソンの話」(*The Story of Samuel Johnson*) として，彼の略伝が紹介されているし（Pp.125-130.），彼の格言も付記されている。(Pp.68, 130, 203.)

40．C-1（1892：明治25年）
　　雄峯高橋光威訳述　貧児立身伝　東京　新進堂発兌　明治25年（初版）
41．C-2（1902：明治35年）
　　増田藤之助編　英語文章軌範　東京専門学校出版部蔵版　明治35年
42．C-3（1912：明治45年）
　　高橋五郎訳　世界文豪　交友観　*THE GIFT OF FRIENDSHIP*　東京　内外出版協会　明治35年（初版）

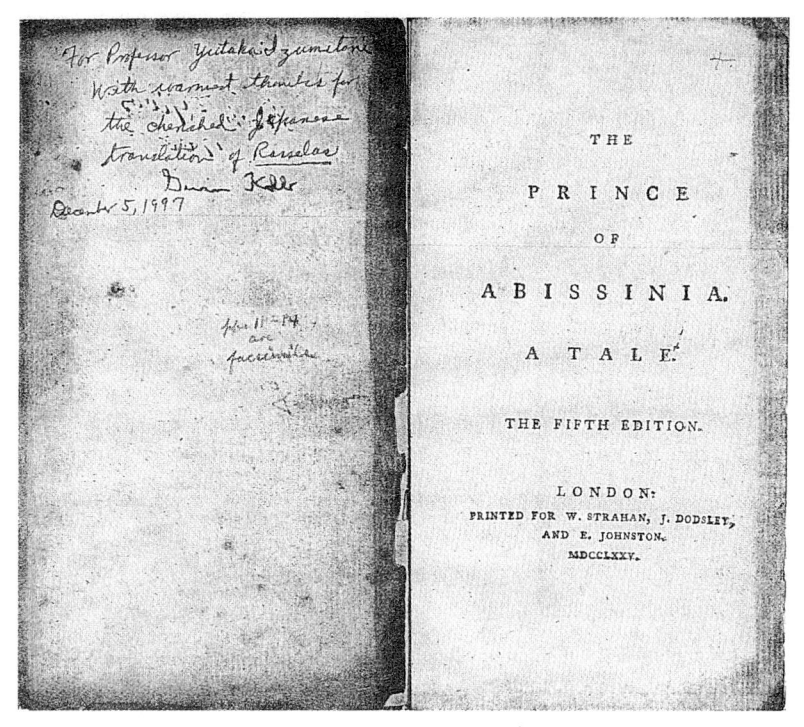

A−1 (1775：安永4年)

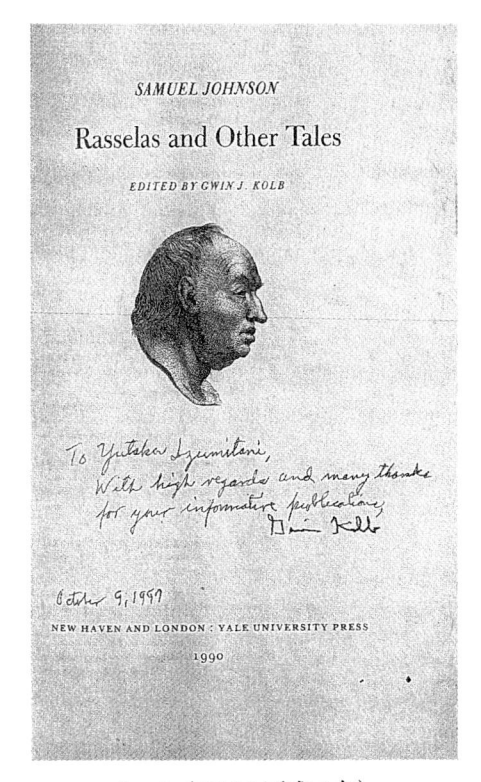

A−2 (1990：平成2年)

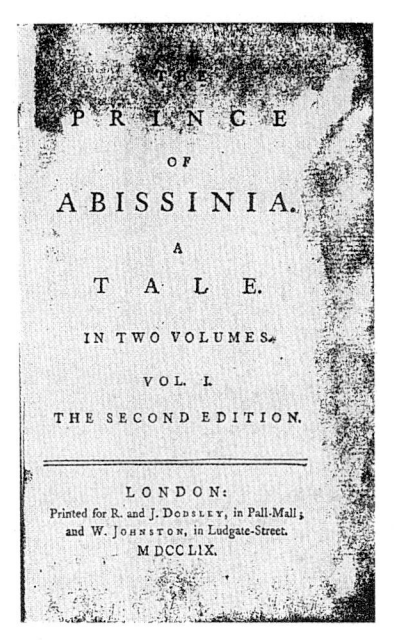

B-1 (1759：宝暦9年, 2nd Edn.)

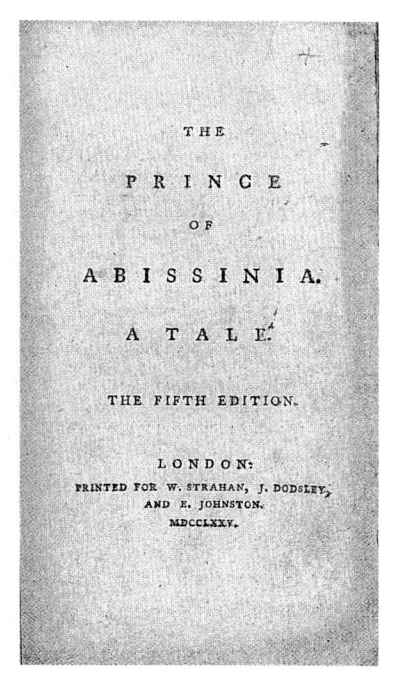

B-2 (1775：安永4年, 5th Edn.)

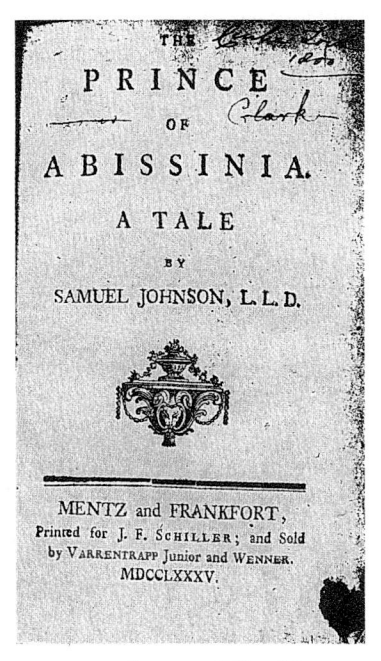

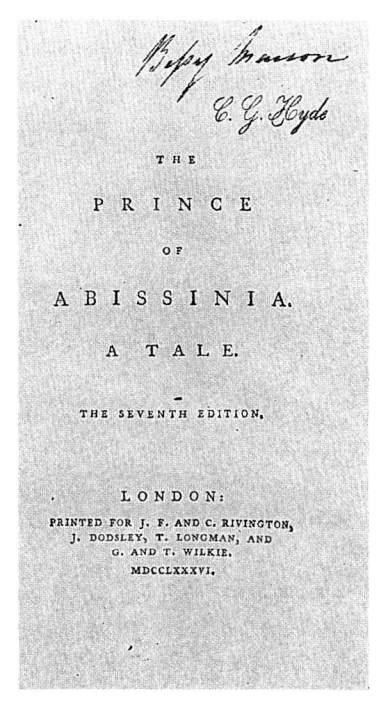

B-3 (1785：天明5年)

B-4 (1786：安永6年, 7th Edn.)

B-5 (1787:天明7年)

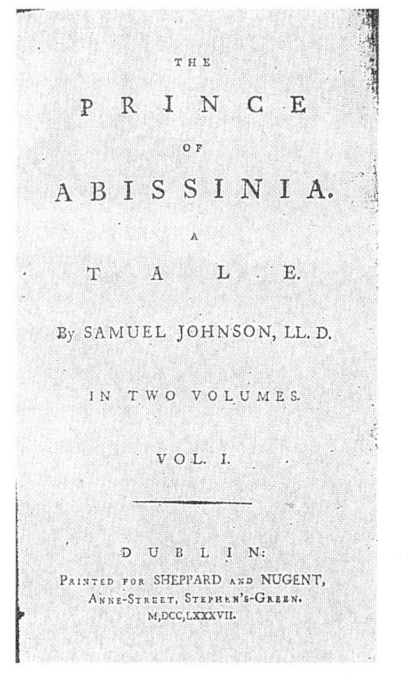

B-6 (1787:天明7年)

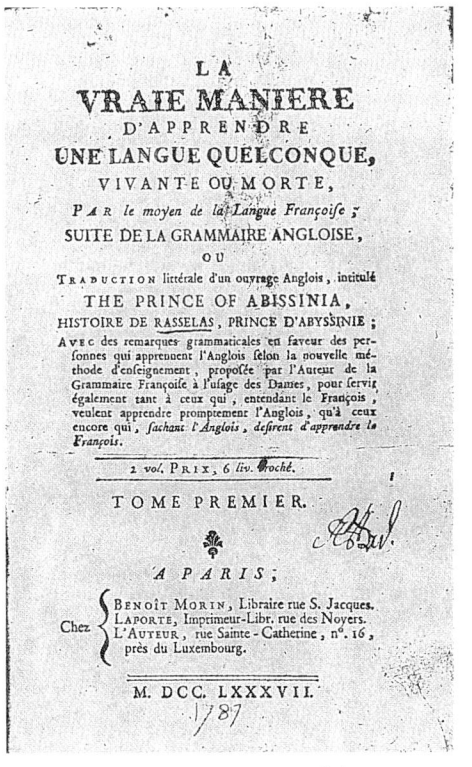

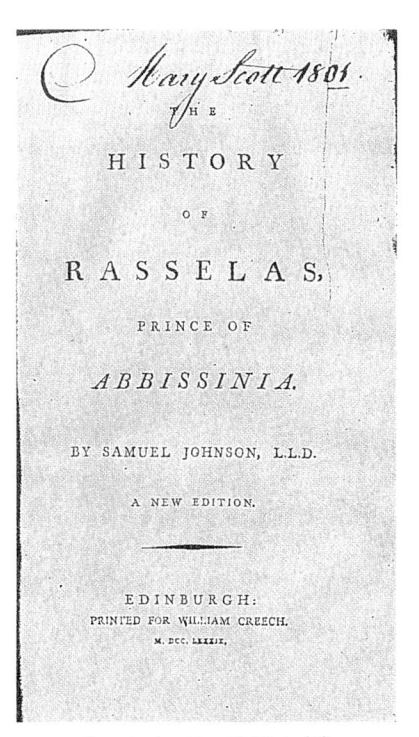

B-7 (1787:天明7年)

B-8 (1789:寛政1年)

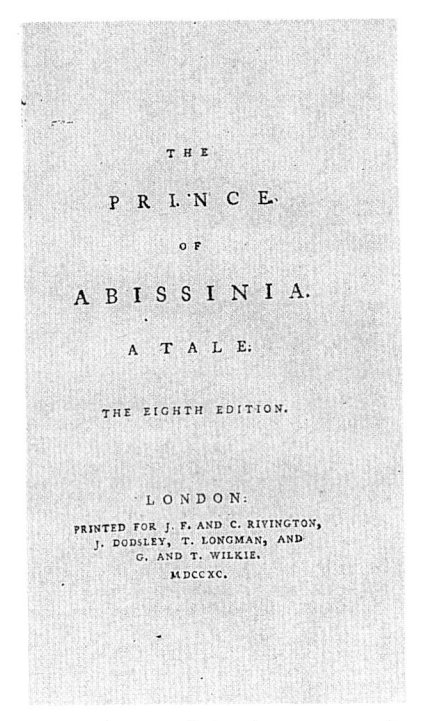

B−9 (1790：寛政2年, 8th Edn.)

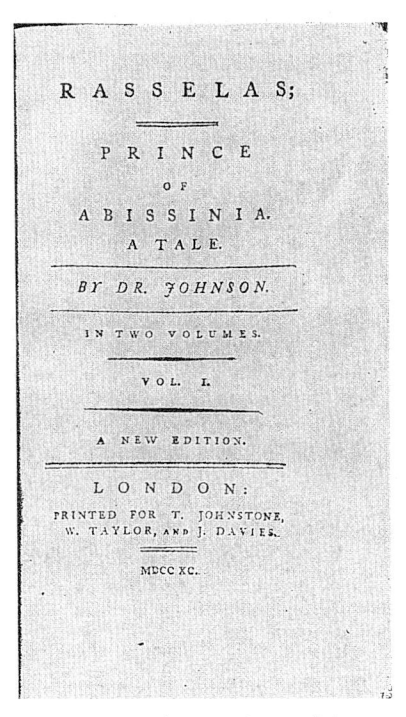

B−10 (1790：寛政2年)

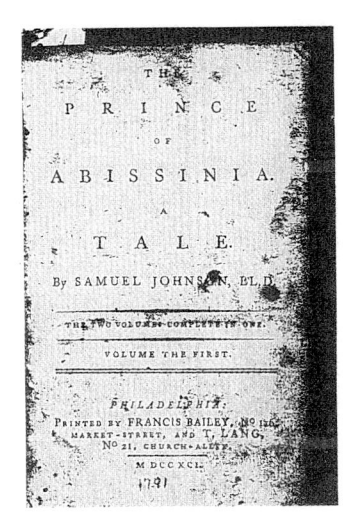

B−11 (1791：寛政3年, USA Edn.)

B−12 (1792：寛政4年)

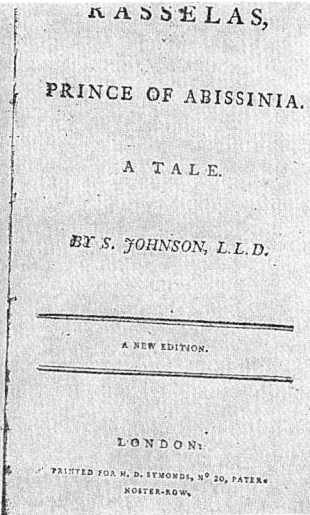

B－13（1795：寛政7年）

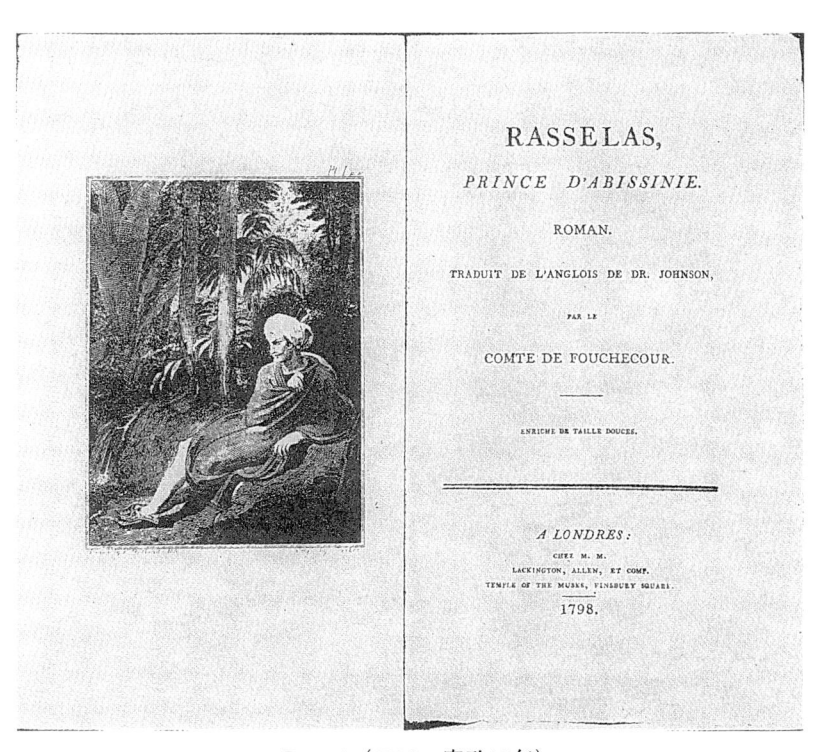

B－14（1798：寛政10年）

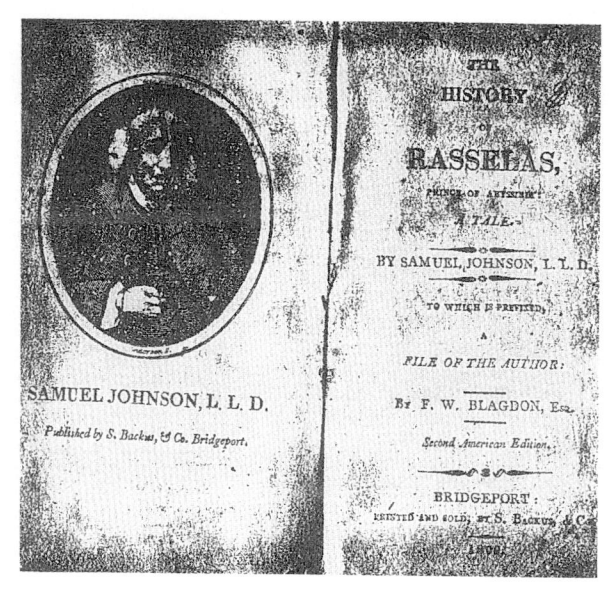

B－15（1800：寛政12年）

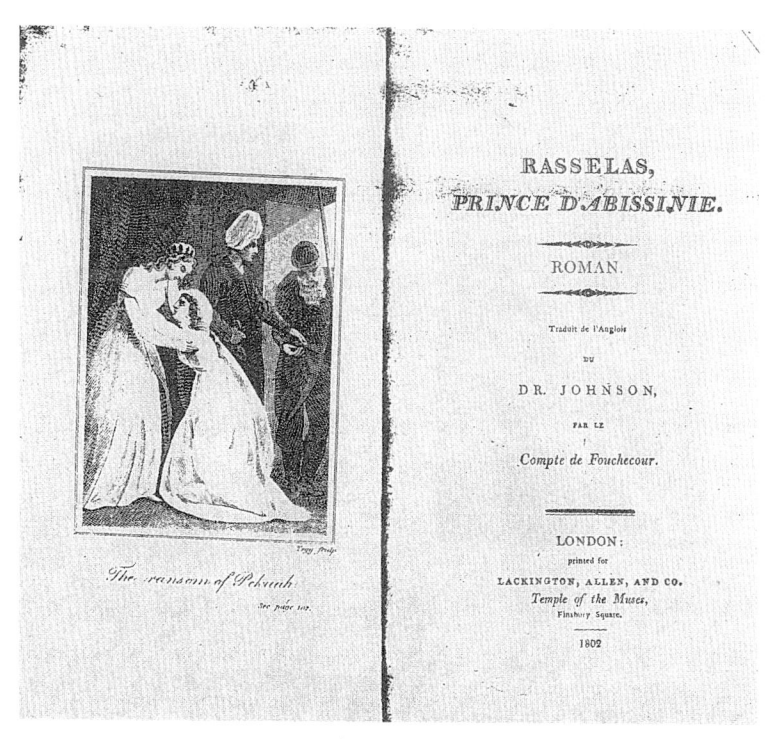

B－16（1802：享和2年）

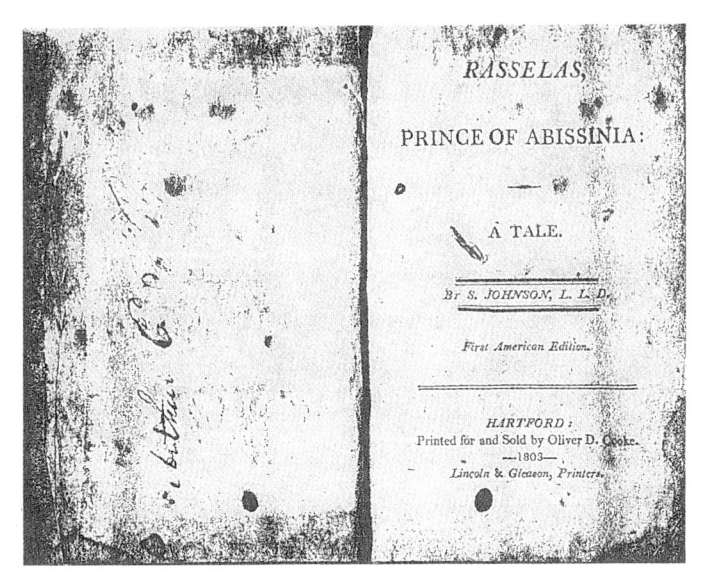

B-17 (1803：享和3年)

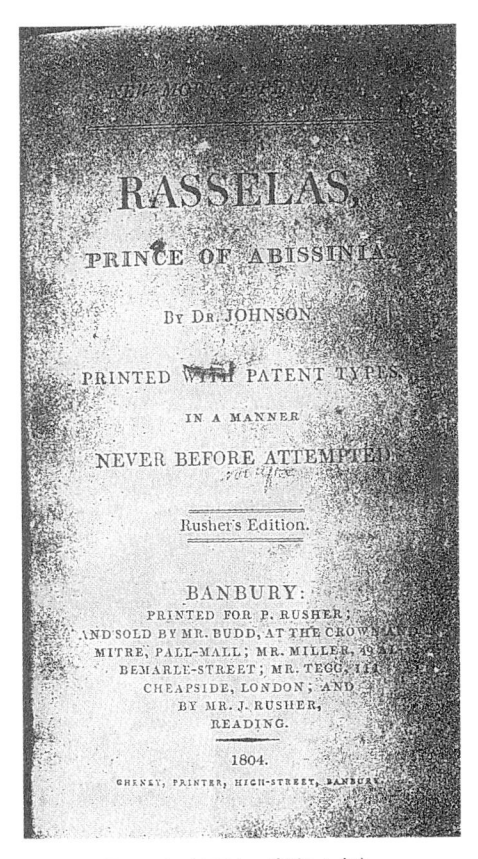

B-18 (1804：享和4年)

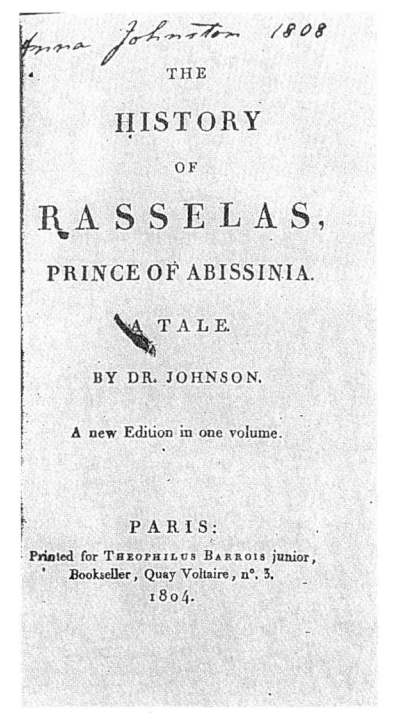

B-19 (1804：享和4年)

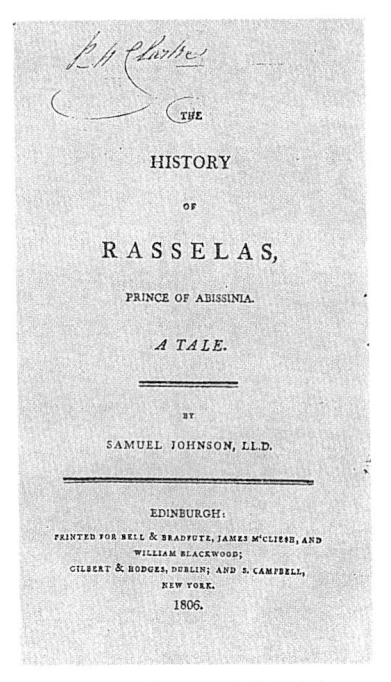

B−20 (1806：文化3年)

B−21 (1809：文化6年)

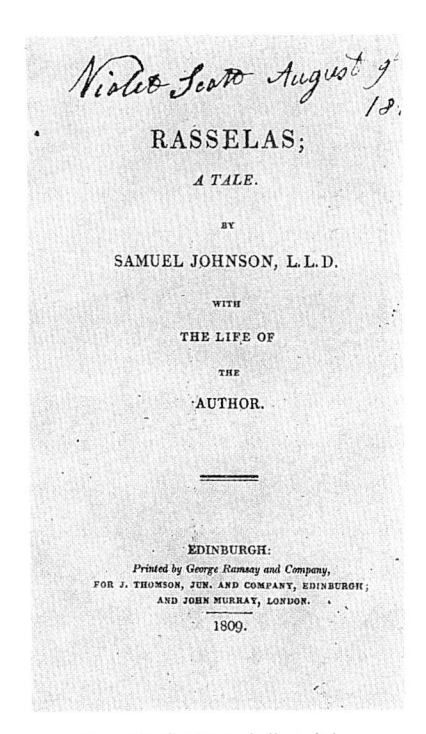

B−22 (1809：文化6年)

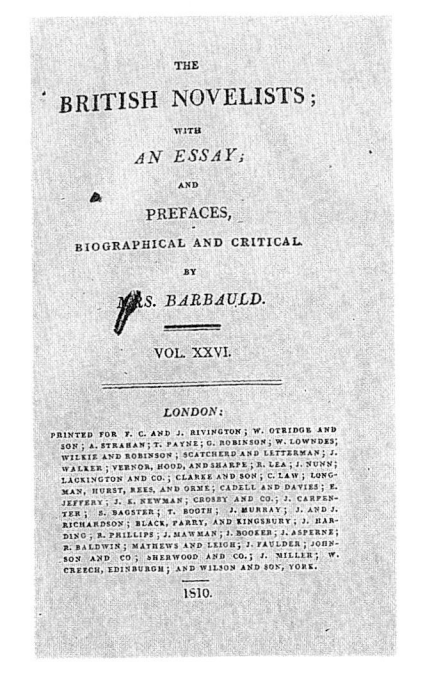

B−23 (1810：文化7年)

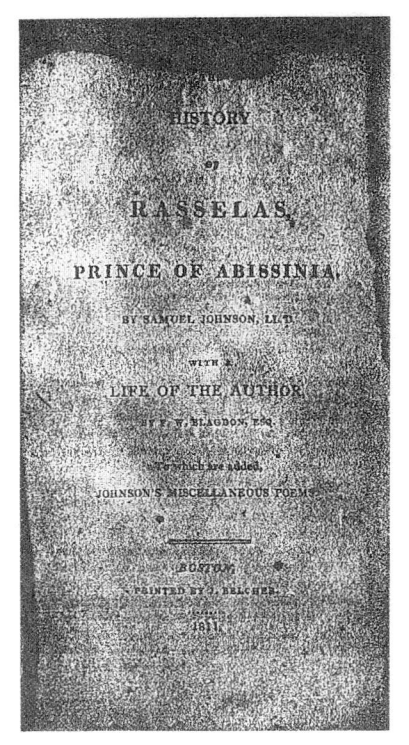

B−24 (1811:文化8年)

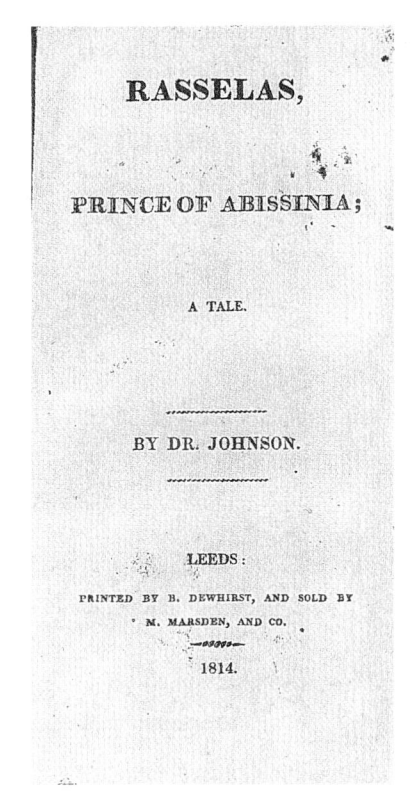

B−25 (1814:享和11年)

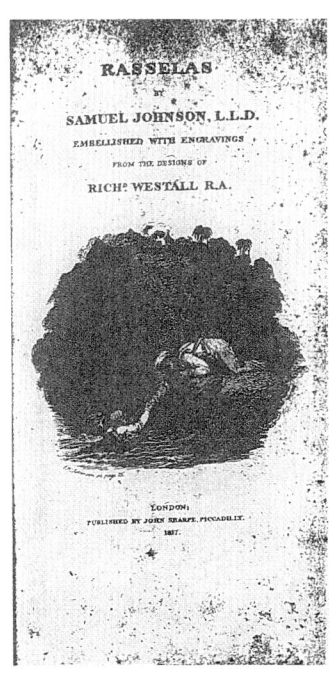

B−26 (1816:文化13年)

B−27 (1817:享保2年)

B-28 (1818：文政1年)

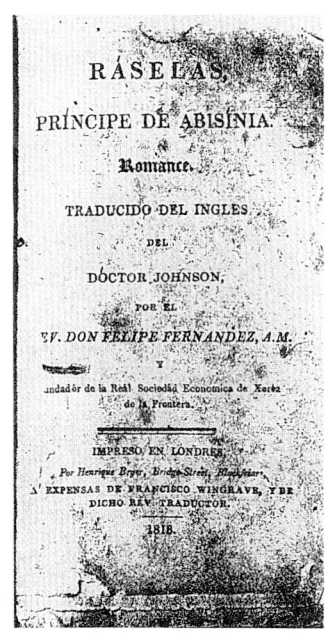

B-29 (1818：文政1年)

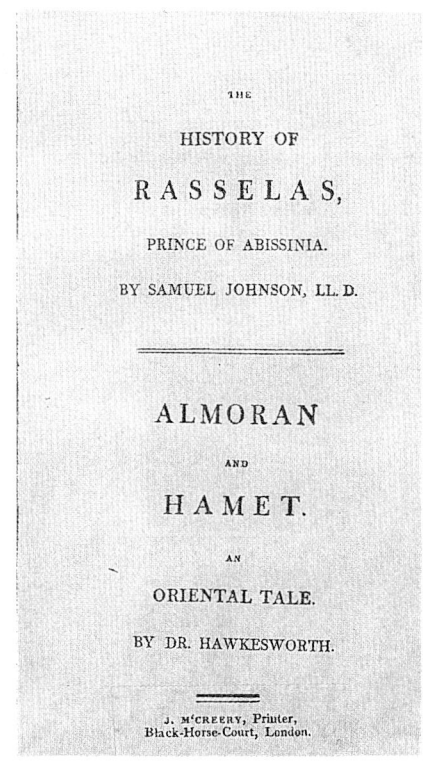

B-30 (1820：文政3年)

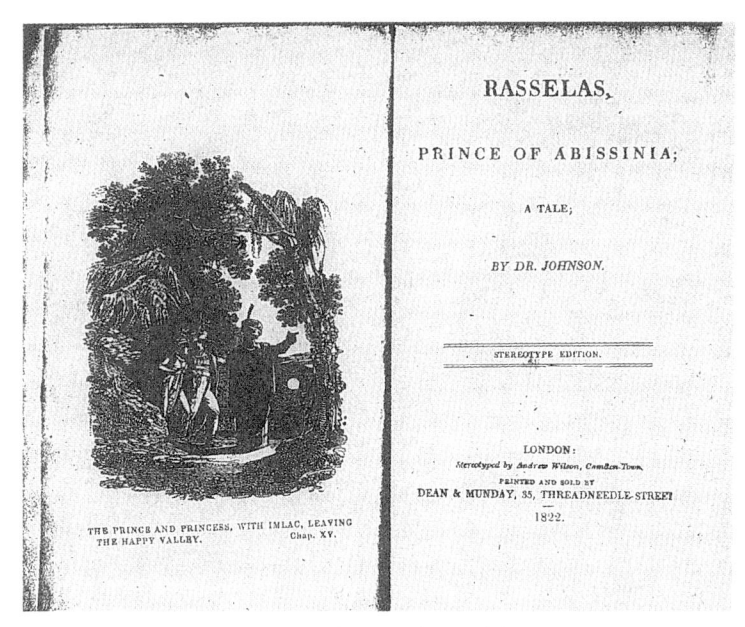

B−31 (1822：文政5年)

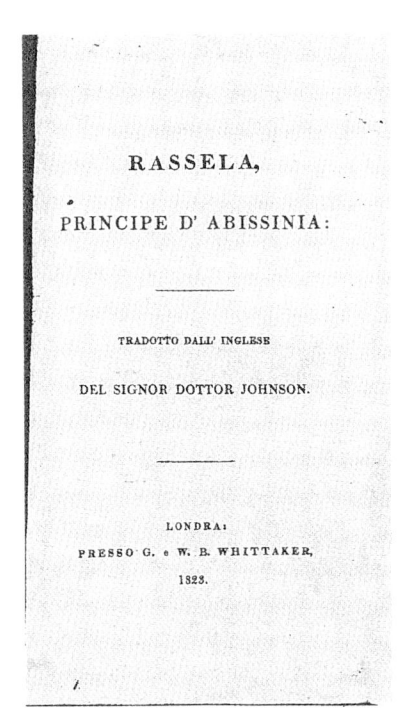

B−32 (1823：文政6年)

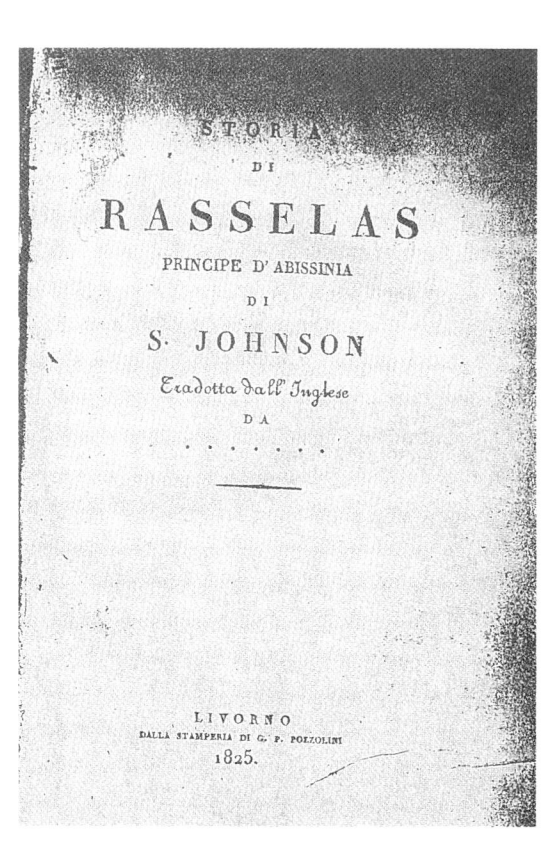

B−33 (1825：文政8年)

B−34（1846：弘化3年）

B−35（N.D. COOKE'S Edn.）

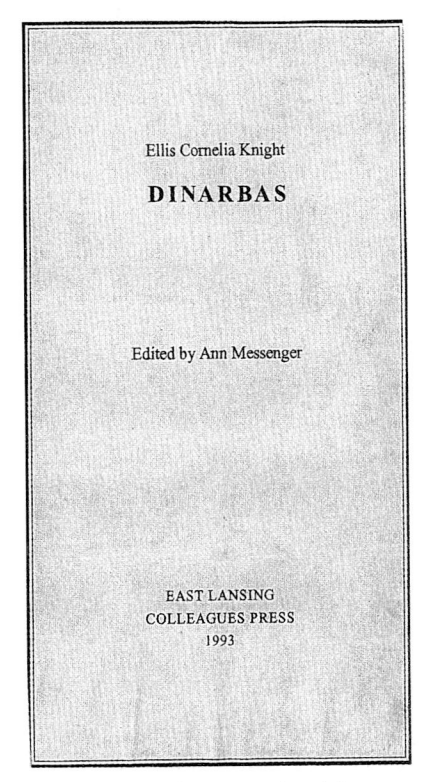

B−36（1993：平成5年）

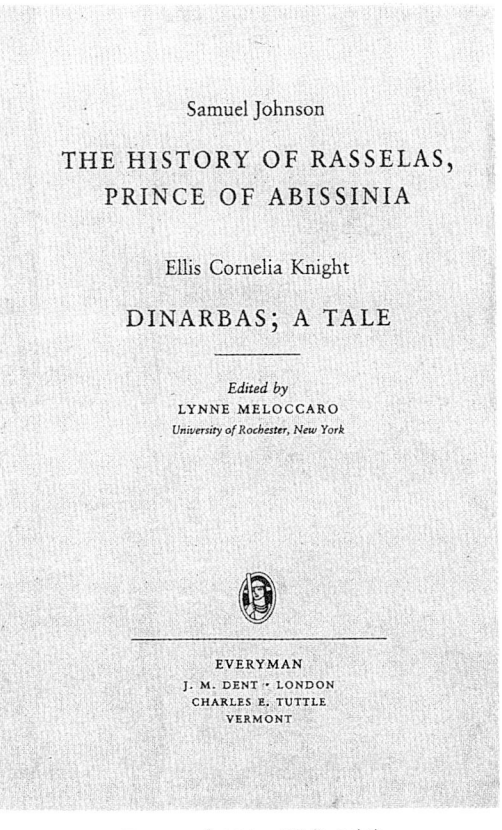

B−37（1994：平成6年）

C−1 (1892：明治25年) 貧兒立身傳　雄峯高橋光威譯述　東京 新進堂發兌

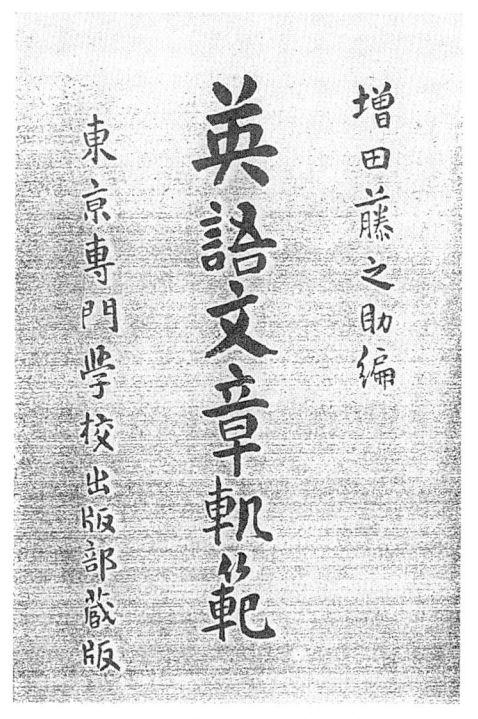

C−2 (1902：明治35年) 英語文章軌範　増田藤之助編　東京專門學校出版部藏版

C−3 (1912：明治45年)

THE GIFT OF FRIENDSHIP.

高橋五郎譯
世界文豪 交友觀
東京 内外出版協會

『ラセラス』受容史の研究(5)

The Reception-History of *Rasselas* (5)

 This paper is the fifth instalment of the serial *The Reception-History of Rasselas*, in which the present writer has been trying to elucidate the influences of S. Johnson's *Rasselas* upon audiences over the past 240 years after its publication of 1759. In this issue, firstly, the third sequel to *Rasselas* by a precocious girl in 1869, which was recently discovered, is introduced to the Japanese readership in some detail. Next, in sections 2, and 3, the writer presents *Happy Valley* and Johnson's House. Section 4 deals with the one book published toward the end of the 18th century from the point of reader-response criticism. The 5th section traces in a cursory manner the classical topos, *Choice* theme. In section 6, Johnson's oriental tales before and after *Rasselas* are outlined: it is noted that little attention has been paid to the interrelations between *Rasselas* and *Almoran and Hamet* by Hawkesworth. Lastly, the paper also calls attention to *The History of Buddha* as a kind of oriental tale.

Keywords : E. Hodgkin, *Happy Valley*, Johnson's House, Addison, Choice, *Rasselas*, Hawkesworth, Buddha

 本稿は，一連の「『ラセラス』受容史の研究」の第5弾として，ジョンソンの物した一編の東洋物語の影響の一端を検討してみたものである。本号では，まず最近発見された一少女による『ラセラス』の続編について，可能なかぎり，詳細に紹介してみた。続いて『ラセラス』と関わるさまざまな問題点について一考しておいた。(2)では，〈幸福の谷〉，(3)では『ラセラス』の書かれたジョンソンの家，(4)においては，十八世紀末頃に出版された一冊の児

童書を紹介した後，(5)では，選択のテーマについて検討してみた。次いで，ジョンソンの東洋物語への関心について触れ，(7)では，ホークスワスの『アルモランとハメト』との関係に注目し，最後の(8)では，釈迦伝が東洋物語として読みうることを指摘しておいた。

I．E. ホジキン作『「ラセラス」の続編』について

　ジョンソンの『ラセラス』（Samuel Johnson, *The History of Rasselas, Prince of Abyssinia*, 1759）は当初の作者自身の意図にもかかわらず，ジョンソン自身によってではなく，2人の教養ある女性によって，その続編が書かれたことは既にご承知のとおりである。すなわち，エリス・コルネリア・ナイトの『ディナバス』（Ellis Cornelia Knight, *Dinarbas, A Tale : Being a Continuation of Rasselas, Prince of Abyssinia*, 1790）とエリザベス・ポープ・ウエイトリィの『「ラセラス」第2部』（Elizabeth Pope Whately, *The Second Part of the History of Rasselas, Prince of Abyssinia*, 1834, 35）である。(拙稿「ラセラスはどこへ帰ったか」，英語青年，May 1，1994，47-48；「ラセラスはどこへ帰ったか — *Dinarbas* をよむ」，『日本ジョンソン協会会報』，May 1993，18-23；「ミセス・ウエイトリ作『ラセラス』第二部について」，『18世紀英文学研究』，雄松堂出版，1996，pp.43-56．参照)。しかし，さらなる続編がエレン・ホジキンというわずか17歳の敬虔聡明な少女によって書かれていたことが，最新の英国ジョンソン協会会報に報じられている。(THE TRANSACTIONS OF JOHNSON SOCIETY, 1998, ed. Alethea Reazon Acasio Malley, pp.34-46)。先の2編については，すでに一考したので，ここではまず第3番目の続編について，ご紹介することから始めてみたい。

　エレン・ホジキン作『「ラセラス」の続編』（Ellen Hodgkin, *A Continuation of the History of Rasselas, Prince of Abyssinia*, Christmas 1869）はわずか2章のみの小品（a piece）であって，1編の物語として公刊するにはあまりにも短く，そのプロットもシンプルという他はないが，にもかかわらず，ジョンソンの『ラセラス』に深く感動し，その結末なき結末（The Conclusion, in Which Nothing is Concluded）に彼女なりの結末をつけずにはおれなかったために，クリスマス当日，あるいはその前後に一挙に書きあげたものと思われる。事実，最終的には『ラセラス』の主人公はアビシニアの王となり，善政よく国運の隆盛をもたらすのである。

　King Rasselas reigned long & prosperously & the great and noble deeds of the mighty potentate & his sister the Prince Nekayah have been handed down as examples of wisdom & princely magnificence to a grateful and revering posterity. (p.45)

　彼女の物語の第1章（Chap I : The Inundation of the Nile Ceases）では，ナイル河（the father of waters）の洪水が予想外にひどく被害がカイロにまで広がっていて，若き主人公たちは幸福探求の挫折に加えて新たな失意と恐怖を引き起こしている。賢者イムラックはよく若者たちを諭し，ラセラスはナイルの水位がかすかに下がりつつあるのを察知して帰国への希望を新たにする。第2章（Chap II : The Prince & Princess with their Followers leave Cairo and proceed upon their Journey）では，よき友人となった天文学者はその知識によって，水嵩の下がるのを予告する。彼はまた一行のアビシニア帰国に同伴を願いでて王子王女を喜ばせる。2人もまた，この善良な友人とは別れたくなかったのである。洪水の難関を越えた一行はいよいよ繁栄の大都カイロ（the great city of Cairo) を後にして，アビシニアの領地にはいっていく。その経過において，若者たちの内にはカイロで見た世俗の幸せ (the outer world happiness) ではなく，強く神 (Providence) を意識した精神的な幸せ ('mental welfare, as well as happiness', p.40) へと導かれていく。無事国境を過ぎ父王の領地にはいった一行は会う人々が一様に悲しみにくれていることに驚く。

Our wise & just King lies dead in yonder palace, & there is no heir to fill the vacant throne. (p.44)

国王葬儀の参列に加わって王宮にはいった一行は王の棺に達したとき，ラセラスは俄然立って並みいる人々に次のように話しかけるのである。

"People of Abyssinia, you have come to gaze in mute respect upon the remains of yr. mighty King who has ruled you wisely & justly for so many years; you mourn also the want of a successor & you dread the rebellions & disturbances which follow upon such a want; behold in me the son of your late King, & one who from much experience in the ways of the world has the knowledge as well as the desire to be the worthy monarch of so great & worthy a people." (p.45)

立派に成長したラセラスに群衆が疑い，驚き，かつ歓喜する。イムラックが一行の冒険の始終を説明してラセラスの正体を証明する。アビシニア国民がこの喜びの確かなことに再び歓声の声を一にするのである。そして先に引用したハッピー・エンディングに終わっている。

著者 Ellen Hodgkin は1852年6月12日に由緒ある敬虔なクェーカー教徒 (the Society of Friends) の家庭に生まれ，1874年9月13日に享年22歳の若さでこの世を去っている。この可憐な少女 ('a beautiful and talented Nelly') の薄命の生涯を思うとあわれという他はない。

今日，われわれがこの物語をよむとき，いくつかの矛盾にも気づかされる。第4王子であったはずのラセラスがこうも安易に王位につくことができたのか，等々。

しかし，これは私の関心事ではない。メッドーフ (Dr. Robert F. Metzdorf, Harvard) も言うように，『ラセラス』はむずかしい本である。("Johnson's *Rasselas* left his readers with several unanswered philosophical questions. It was a book to make people think; not merely a slight Oriental tale, hastily written to pay the funeral expenses of the author's mother." *The New Rambler,* January 1950, 5-7.) 当時の少年少女たちが読み耽ったアラビアン・ナイト (*Arabian Nights*) や，妖怪 (genii, fairies) の出没する他の東洋物語とも違ったこの難解な本に捕らわれて，真剣に人生を考え，至上なるものに想いを馳せつつ，なお真の幸せを追い求めずにはおれなかったかの国の過去の少女たちのことである。(Cf. Hannah More, *The Search for Happiness*, 1766.) イギリス小説のうちには『ラセラス』をよむ主人公たちがよく登場する。まず，想起されるのがヘレン バーンズ (Helen Burns) である。(C. Bronte, *Jane Eyre*, 1847, ch. 5) また，ジョージ・エリオットの『牧師館物語』(George Eliot, *Scenes from Clerical Life*, 1858, ch.3) のメアリー・ジャネット (Mary Janet) であり，『フロス河の水車小屋』(*The Mill on the Floss*, 1860, ch. 3) のマギー・ツリバー (Maggie Tulliver) である。さらに，ジェーン・オースティンの『マンスフィールド・パーク』(Jane Austin, *Mansfield Park*, esp. ch. 26) に登場するファニー・プライス (Fanny

Price）である。また，"I prefer Dr. Johnson to Mr. Boz." と言って，イムラックとラセラスの会話の1節を高らかに朗読したジェンキンズ嬢（Miss Jenkyns）である。(Mrs Gaskell, *Cranford*, 1851-3, ch. 1）そして，その背後にいる，これらの作品を書いた作家自身の真剣に読書する10代の姿である。マコーレー（T. B. Macaulay）の言葉を借りれば，Miss Lydia Languish（Butler SheridanのRivalの主人公）タイプの少女たちとは縁のない彼女たちである（See. *Samuel Johnson*, 1856）。「君はジョンソンの『ラセラス』を知っているかね？ ぜひ一度読んでみたまえ，そして君の感想を聞かせてほしいものだ。」1827年，ゲーテは若きエッカーマンにこう述べている（『ゲーテとの対話』(上)，岩波文庫，1993，p.324）。しかし，両者はその後に何のコメントもしていない。この不可思議なジョンソンの物語には彼等も断言することができなかったものと思われる。

1．A－1（1869：明治2年）
 Ellen Hodgkin, *A Continuation of the History of Rasselas, Prince of Abyssinia* (Christmas 1869)

II．〈幸福の谷〉について

〈幸福の谷〉（The Happy Valley）については，本稿(2)C－7においてR. W. Dessaiの見取図を紹介しておいた。ジョンソンはこの着想をLuis de Urreta's *Historia Ecclesiastica, Politica, Natural y Moral de los Grandes y Remotos Reynos de la Etiopia* (Valencia, 1610) から得たものとも思われるが，同時に郷里リッチフィールド（Lichfield）の郊外の田園風景をイメージしていたとも言われている。(BBC Video,' Samuel Johnson.' Happy Valleyの詳細については，Kolb, Introduction, pp. xxvi-xxxi 参照）。ジョンソンを敬愛したホーソン（Nathaniel Hawthorn）は母校Harley Collegeをthe Happy Valleyに例えて，次のように述べている。

The local situation of the College, so far secluded from the sight and sound of the busy world, is peculiarly favorable to the moral, if not to the literary habits of its students; and this advantage probably caused the founders to overlook the inconveniences that were inseparably connected with it. The humble edifices rear themselves almost at the farthest extremity of a narrow vale, which, winding through a long extent of hill-country, is well nigh as inaccessible, except at the one point, as the Happy Valley of Abyssinia.(*Fanshawe*, 1st edn., 1828.)

また，彼はリヴァプール領事時代（1853-7）にLichfield, Uttoxeterへ旅して，その記録や作品を残している。(See *Biographical Stories*, 1842; *Our Old Town*, 1863; *The English Note-books*, 1870.) アメリカにおける他の作家たちへのジョンソンの影響やその受容については，「ジョンソンとアメリカ」を特集した，*The Age of Johnson; A Scholarly Annual* 6,(ed. Paul J. Korshin, AMS PRESS, Inc. 1994.), とりわけ，James G. Basker, "Samuel Johnson and the American Common Reader" (3-30)を参照されたい。さらに，『ラセラス』を愛読したベックフォード（William Beckford, 1760-1844）の『ヴァテック』（*Vathek*, 1786）冒頭の五つの宮殿（five palaces）や，Hall of Eblisはやや異質ではあるが，ジョンソンの幸福の谷を連想させられる。("As an Eastern tale, even *Rasselas* must bow before it(i. e. *Vathek*): his 'happy valley' will not bear a comparison with the 'Hall of Eblis.'" M. P. Conant, pp.258-259.)

2．B－1（1830：文政13年）
　The engraving in tint from original designs by Devereux in *The History of Rasselas, Prince of Abissinia*, Philadelphia: Hogan & Thompson, 1893.
3．B－2（1828：文政11年）
　FANSHAWE, A TALE／BOSTON:MARSH & CAPEN, 362 WASHINGTON STREET.／PRESS OF PUTMAN AND HUNT.／1828.

Ⅲ．『ラセラス』の家

　1737年の上京以来，ジョンソンはロンドンで17箇所ほど住居を変えたが，今日唯一残されているゴフ・スクエア（Gough Square）17番地は1746年頃から1759年3月頃までの最も多産な時代の住居となった所である。『ラセラス』もこの家において書かれている。この家は1700年頃，ゴフという名のロンドンの長老によって建てられたと言われている。1911年，住み荒らされていた家は初代ハームズワス卿によって買い取られて今日に至っている。現在は Dr. Johnson's House Trust（Chairman: the Lord Harmsworth）によって管理運営されている。
4．C－1　Johnson's House（創建 *c*.1700：元禄13年頃）

Ⅳ．アジソン編『道徳雑纂集』について

　18世紀後半のイギリス読書界においては，東洋物語やこれに類する教訓的，あるいは道徳的な出版物が流行し，おびただしい数の児童用書物が刊行されている。当時の読書する少年少女たちの趣好も分かるので，代表的な1冊を挙げておきたい。原題は，アジソン氏編纂『興味ある逸話，追憶，アレゴリー，随想，さらに，詩篇を提供して想像力を楽しませ，併せて道義心を啓蒙する』（1794）である。
　この書物には目次もないが，書中の作品を数えてみると，逸話（Anecdotes）39篇，追憶（Memoirs）2篇，詩篇（Verses）15篇，訓話（Essays）14篇，小話（Stories）32，アレゴリー（Allegories）2篇，東洋物語（Oriental tales）3篇，合計107篇である。東洋物語そのものは少ないが逸話その他にも題材を東洋の国々においている。また，ジョンソンの作品も取り入れられているし，彼の逸話も紹介されている。（pp. 24-31；102-110, 161, 162, 237-241, 242-249.）まさに，彼等の想像力は "From Britain to Japan"（p.269）へと東洋の方向に向けられていたのである。（金子健二著『東洋思想の西漸と英吉利文学』，昭和9年3月，印刷者　西川喜右衛門，pp.225-228，参照）。しかし，現実的に彼等の勢力が東洋に延び拡大し，オリエント研究も本格化するのに反比例して，東洋物語は衰微していくことになる。
5．D－1（1794：寛政6年）
　INTERESTING／ANECDOTES, MEMOIRES,／ALLEGORIES, ESSAYS,／AND／POETICAL FRAGMENTS;／TENDING／TO AMUSE THE FANCY, AND INCULCATE／MORALITY.／BY MR. ADDISON.／LONDON:／PRINTED FOR THE AUTHOR／1794.

Ⅴ．〈選択〉（Choice）について

　古来，西欧人の精神思考を形づくってきたものにこの〈選択〉がある。わけても，18世紀にはこの古典文学のトポスが文学の主題とも結びついて，さまざまな作品を生み出している。『ラセラス』に限らずジョンソンの他の作品もそうである。人生には人さまざまな形の戦いが用意されている。

われわれは1本の道ではなく，2本（あるいは3本）のわかれ道に立って，決断しなければならない。自由意志によるこのような弁証法的上昇思考によって主体的に選択する生き方の呪文から解放されるのはカーライル（Thomas Carlyle, 1795-1881. *Sartor Resartus* 参照）の時代になってからではないだろうか。王子のように豊かな選択肢のある生き方のできない者もあろう。選択は能動的な態だけでなく，選択されるという受動態ともなる。また，選択することは他を捨てることであるから，豊かな生き方の放棄ともなろう。実に選択のもつ意味は大きいのである。われわれには簡択断疑（けんじゃくだんぎ）という言葉がある。択び，もっと択んで疑いを断じるところに知恵が生まれるの意味である。また，『あなたがたはわかれ道に立って，よく見，いにしえの道につき，良い道がどれかを尋ねて，その道を歩み，そしてあなたがたの魂のために安息を得よ。』という「エレミヤ書」第6章16節の聖句や天をめざすヤコブの夢（「創世記」第12-3節）が想起される。万学の父アリストテレスのジョンソンに対する影響，とりわけ『ニコマコス倫理学』（*The Nicomachean Ethics*）へのジョンソンの愛着ぶりに注目したい。彼の数少ない虚構の作品はこのカテゴリー内で書かれたように思われる。参考箇所としては次のようなものがある。

Cicero, *De Officiis*, i.32-33 (115, 117, 119); Plato, *Republic*, ix.7(581C), x.15(617D); Aristotle, *Ethics*, i.5; Cicero, *Tusculanae Disputationes*, v.3(8-9); Macrobius, *Commentariorum in Somnium Scipionis*, ii.17.

なお，E－9は大正期に活躍し，昭和2年に41歳で亡くなった万鉄五郎の墨画である。俯瞰構図による本作品では道が川のように流れて心地よい南画である。また，菊池寛には三筋の別れ道を各自歩んだ「三人兄弟」の話がある。（桑原三郎・千葉俊二編『日本児童文学名作集』（下），岩波文庫，pp.17-39.）前号(4)，p.156で触れた SANDERS' UNION FOURTH READER: BY CHARLES W. SANDERS, M. A., (NEW YORK AND CHICAGO: Ivison, Blakeman & Co., 1863), pp.237-240 に採用されている3姉妹のアレゴリーが思い出される。紹介した版図は主として E. C. Heinle の *The Eighteenth Century Allegorical Essay* (1957) に付されたものからお借りした。詳細については，同書および拙訳「ピナックス：人生の絵姿」（四国学院大学『論集』，1992. 7, pp.81-104）の解説を参照されたい。

6．E－1（1509：永正7年）

　In *The ship of fools* by Alexander Barclay

7．E－2（ND）

　Tabura Cebetis. From N. K. Farmer, Jr., *Poets and the Visual Arts in Renaissance England*, p.21.)

8．E－3（1618：元和2年）

　Emblemata by Andreae Alciati (Paris, 1618), p.80.

9．E－4（1521：永正19年）

　Cebes by Hans Holbein the Younger (1521)

10．E－5（1635：寛永12年）

　Frontispiece, *A Collection of Emblems* by George Wither (London, 1935)

11．E－6（1672：寛文12年）

　Orbis Sensualium pictus by Johann Comenius (London, 1672), p.221. This Life is a way, or a place divided into,／two ways, like／Pythagoras's letter Y／broad 1.／on the left-hand track,／narrow 2.／on the right;／that belongs to Vice 3.／this to virtue, 4.／Fine, young man, 5.／imitate Hercules.／leave the left-bind way,／turn from vice.

12. E－7 （1714：正徳4年）
    Characteristicks by Shaftbury (London, 1714), vol.Ⅲ.
13. E－8 （1748：寛延1年）
    The Choice of Hercules in *Preceptor* (1748), vol.Ⅱ.
14. E－9 （c.1922：大正11年頃）
    万鉄五郎，わかれ道，76.5×64.6cm，岩手県立博物館

Ⅵ. 『ラセラス』以前以後

東洋に題材を求めた悲劇「アイリーニ」（*Irene*, 1737完稿）を携え，文壇への野望を秘めて上京したジョンソンには，東洋物語への格別の思いがあった。すでに1735年には，ロボの『アビシニア旅行記』（Lobo's *A Voyage to Abyssinia*, 原典はJoachim Le Grand, *Relation historique d'abissinie du R. P. Jerome Lobo*, 1728）を英訳していた。『ラセラス』出版の1759年を「驚異の年」（an annus mirabilis）としてその前後の経緯を簡略してたどっておこう。

1750 （寛延3年）	Hamet and Raschid (*Rambler*, no. 38, July 28.)
1750 （寛延3年）	Obidah, the son of Abensima, and the Hermit (*R.*, no. 65, Oct.)
1751 （宝暦元年）	Nourdin the Merchant and his son Almamoulin (*R.*, no. 120, May 11.)
1752 （宝暦2年）	Mored, the son of Hanuth and his son Abonzaid (*R.*, no. 190, Jan 11.)
1752 （宝暦2年）	Seged, Lord of Ethiopia (*R.*, no. 204, 205, Feb 29, March 3.)
1759 （宝暦9年）	The Prince of Abissinia [*sic*], a Tale
1759 （宝暦9年）	Gelalledin (*Idler*, no. 75, Sept.22.)
1760 （宝暦10年）	Ortogrul of Basra (*I.*, no. 99, March 8.)
1760 （宝暦10年）	Omar, Son of Hassan (*I.*, no. 101, March 22.)

Ⅶ. ホークスワス作『アルモランとハメト』

『ラセラス』に遅れること2年，1761年に出版されたホークスワスの『アルモランとハメト』（John Hawkesworth, *Almoran and Hamet*, 1761）に注目しておきたい。ジョンソンの忠実な模倣者といわれ，また，親交のあったホークスワスのこの東洋物語は『ラセラス』を意識して書かれた好敵手（a rival to *Rasselas*, Thomas Percy's words.）であるのみならず，『ラセラス』以上に東洋物語の特徴を備えた作品である。彼の伝記を書いたアボットの言葉によれば，両書とも「人生の選択と至福達成にいたる手段の哲学的考察」（'the philosophical investigations of the choices life offers and the means by which happiness can be achieved.' John Lawrence Abbott, *John Hawkesworth*, Univ. of Wisconsin Press, 1982, p.114.）である。最後に『アルモランとハメト』第1巻1章冒頭の勧告文（exhortation, injunction, invocation）を引用しておきたい。『ラセラス』冒頭の一節と比較されたい。

Who is he among the children of the earth, that repines at the power of the wicked? and who is he, that would change the lot of the righteous? He, who has appointed to each his portion, is God; the Omniscient and the Almighty, who fills eternity, and whose existence is from Himself! but he who murmurs, is man, who yesterday was not, and who tomorrow shall be forgotten: let him listen in silence to the voice of knowledge, and hide the blushes of confusion in the dust. (*Almoran & Hamet*)

Ye who listen with credulity to the whispers of fancy, and pursue with eagerness the phantoms of hope; who expect that age will perform the promises of youth, and that the deficiences of the present day will be supplied by the morrow; attend to the history of Rasselas prince of Abissinia. (*Rasselas*)

Ⅷ. 釈迦伝と『ラセラス』

　最近，英・仏両文によるささやかな釈迦伝を一読したとき，ジョンソンの『ラセラス』（Samuel Johnson, *The History of Rasselas, Prince of Abissinia*, 1759）の主人公たちを連想するとともに，あたかも，1篇の東洋物語（Oriental tales）を読んでいるかのような錯覚を覚えた。釈迦の生涯の物語（history）は18世紀イギリスの読者には彼等の愛読した東洋物語の1篇として通用するのみならず，それ相応の感銘を聡明な少年少女たちに与えたに違いないという感想を持った。また，ジョンソンの『ラセラス』では若き主人公たちの人生の選択が竜頭蛇尾な結果に終わったことから，過去240年におよんで読者をも満足させるハッピー・エンディングを意図して，さまざまな論争をも引き起こしてきた。また，その続編が現に3人の教養ある女性によって書かれていることも先に指摘したとおりである。これらの女性によって書かれた作品はいずれも神の節理（Providence）による永遠の選択（the Choice of Eternity）に心魂の喜びを与えられ，同時に現世のしあわせをも実現している。現世の不幸不安に苦しみ，城をでて，試練ののち確かな結論に達した釈迦の物語と十分な結末に達しえなかった王子ラセラスとの2人の王子の選択，とりわけ永遠の選択（The Choice of Eternity）については興味ある課題と思われる。

　ご承知のとおり，ゴータマ・ブッダ（Gautama Buddha，紀元前5－4世紀頃）は釈迦族の王シュッドーダナ（Shuddhodana Gautama，浄飯）の王子として生まれ，19歳で結婚，10年の間王子として生活し，1子ラーフラ（Rahula，羅睺羅）をえた29歳で出家，6年間の試練の後35歳でさとりを開き仏となった。その後，45年間を布教に努め80歳でねはんにはいったと言われている。その選択の結論が不動であったことを示すとともに見事に完結した生涯である。その生涯は多数の仏伝があるにもかかわらず伝説的神秘的叙述に満ちて正確さは期しがたい。それだけに，一層物語ともなりうるものである。一読した釈迦伝とは次の書物である。

BUKKYO DENDO KYOKAI, THE TEACHING OF BUDDHA, L'ENSEIGNEMENT DU BOUDDHA (1966), CHAP. ONE 'The Life of the Buddha,' pp.2-14.

　なお，SJには釈迦や仏教に関する言及はどこにも見られない。中世英文学の作品の中には仏教説話のエコーが見られる由である。（金子健二著『東洋思想の西漸と英吉利文学』（印刷者　西川喜右衛門，昭和9年），305－320頁。

主要参考文献一覧

オリエンタリズムに関する文献は数多く見られるのに比して，東洋物語そのものの文献は意外に少ない。以下筆者の参考したものを中心に掲げておく。

1. Conant, Martha Pike. *The Oriental Tale in England in the Eighteenth Century.* New York: Columbia Univ. Press, 1908. Rpt. Octagon Books, INC., 1966.
2. Ekhtiar, Rochelle Suzette. *Fictions of Enlightenment: The Oriental Tale in the Eighteenth Century England.* Ph.D. diss., Brandeis University, 1985.
3. Heinle, E. C. *The Eighteenth Century Allegorical Essay.* Ph.D. diss. Columbia University, 1957.
4. Marshall, P.J. and Williams, G. *The Great Map of Mankind: British Perceptions of the World in the Age of Enlightenment.* London: Dent, 1982.
5. Parker, Kenneth, ed. *Early Modern Tales of Orient.* London & New York: Routledge, 1999.
6. Weitzman, Arthur J. 'The Oriental Tale in the Eighteenth Century: A Reconsideration,' *Studies on Voltaire and the Eighteenth Century* 58 (1967): 1839-1855.
7. 金子健二著『東洋思想の西漸と英吉利文学』，昭和9年3月，印刷者 西川喜右衛門.

なお，次の各編書に付された序文，解説が有益である。

1. Kolb, Gwin J, ed. *Rasselas and Other Tales.* New Haven & London: Yale Univ. Press, 1990.
2. Mack, Robert L, ed. *Oriental Tales.* Oxford & New York: Oxford Univ. Press, 1992.
3. ——, ed. *Arabian Nights' Entertainments.* Oxford & New York: Oxford Univ. Press, 1995.
4. Meloccaro, Lynne, ed. *Samuel Johnson, The History of Rasselas, Prince of Abissinia and Ellis Cornelia Knight, Dinarbas; A Tale.* London: J.M. Dent & Vermont: Charles E. Tuttle, 1994.

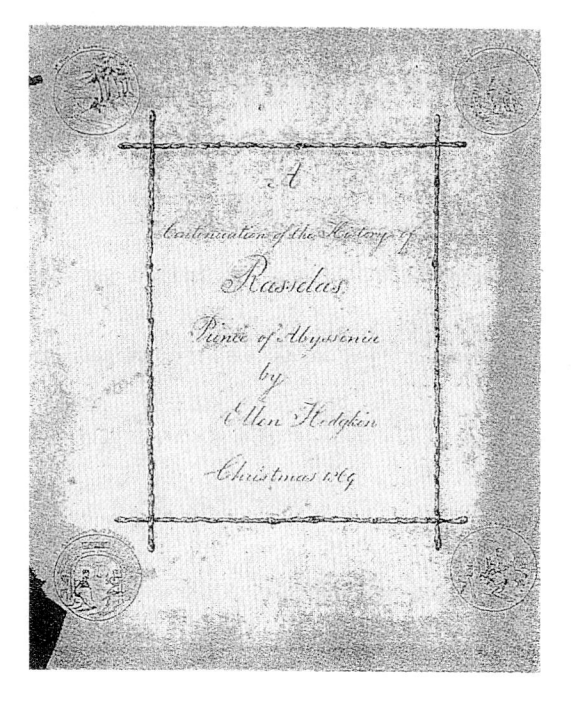

A−1（1869：明治2年）

B−1（1830：文政13年）

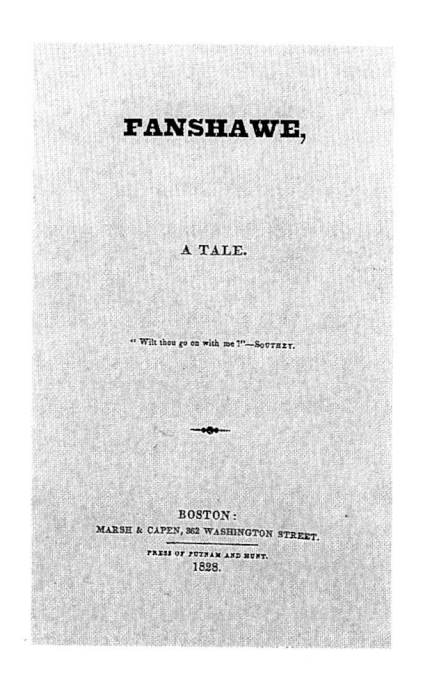

B−2（1828：文政11年）

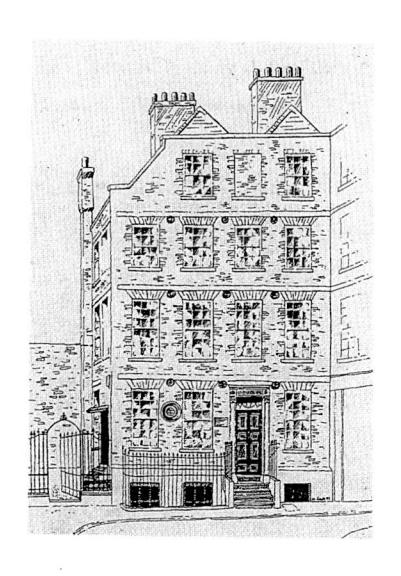

C−1 Johnson's House
　　（創建 *c.*1700：元禄13年頃）

『ラセラス』受容史の研究(5)　　　　　　　　　　105

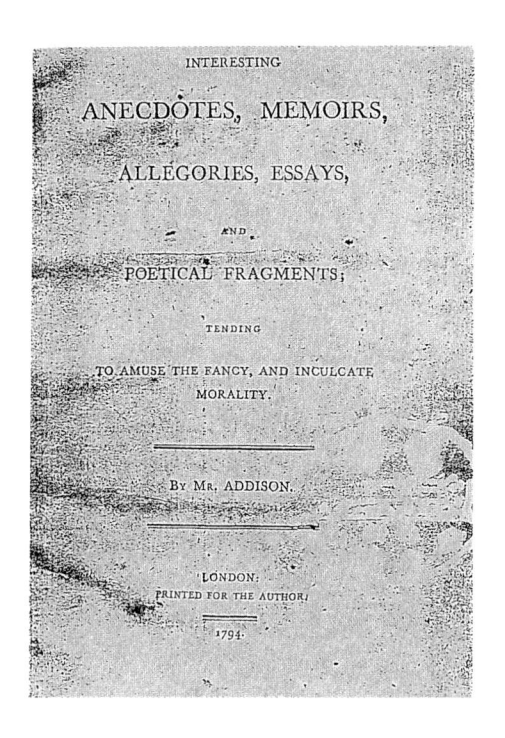

D-1（1794：寛政6年）

E-1（1509：永正7年）

E-2（ND）

E-3（1618：元和4年）

E-4 (1521：永正19年)

E-5 (1635：寛政12年)

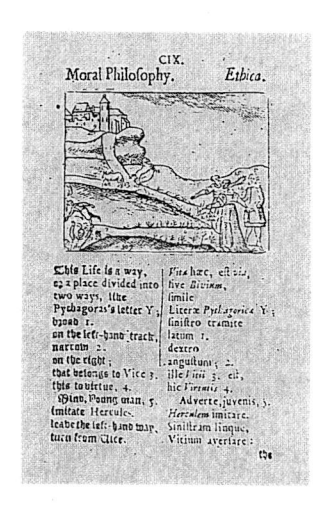

E-6 (1672：寛文12年)

E-7 (1714：正徳4年)

E−8（1748：寛政1年）

E−9（c.1922：大正11年頃）

編者紹介

泉谷　寛（いずみたに・ゆたか）

　1937年旧満州国安東市生まれ（本籍香川県）。早稲田大学第一文学部卒業。岡山大学大学院修士課程修了。1984−85年，ジョージタウン大学大学院，イェール大学大学院研究員。専攻：18世紀英文学，ジョンソンとボズウェル。所属学会：英国ジョンソン協会，日本ジョンソン協会，日本18世紀学会，日本ジョンソン・クラブ，他。現在，広島国際学院大学教授，広島大学総合科学部講師。〈著・訳・編書〉『ある老美人への哀歌』（訳書：私家版，昭和56年），『ジョンソン短編集』（編書：京都・あぽろん社，昭和61年），『人物百態』（編書：京都・あぽろん社，昭和62年），『ジョンソン随想集』（編書：東京・ニューカレント・インターナショナル社，昭和62年），『テネリフの隠者・セオドーの夢』（訳書：京都・あぽろん社，平成3年），『健闘の文豪ジョンソン』（単著：広島・溪水社，平成4年），『ジョンソン研究——その人と作品——』（単著：広島・溪水社，平成5年），『十八世紀イギリス文学研究』（共著：東京・雄松堂出版，平成8年），『永遠の選択——サミュエル・ジョンソン説教集——』（訳書：東京・聖公会出版，平成9年，『サミュエル・ジョンソン百科事典』（共訳：東京・ゆまに書房，平成11年），『「ラセラス」受容史の研究』（編書：広島・溪水社，平成13年）。その他ジョンソン等に関する論文。

『ラセラス』受容史の研究

2001年4月10日　発行

編　者　泉谷　寛
発行所　㈱溪水社
　　　　広島市中区小町1−4　（〒730-0041）
　　　　電　話　（082）246−7909
　　　　Ｆ　Ａ　Ｘ　（082）246−7876
　　　　E-mail: info@keisui.co.jp

ISBN4-87440-643-2　C3098